Charles Dickens on Detectives

Charles Dickens (1812-1870) is regarded by many readers and literary critics to be THE major English novelist of the Victorian Age. He is remembered today as the author of a series of weighty novels which have been translated into many languages and promoted to the rank of World Classics. The latter include, but are not limited to, *The Adventures of Oliver Twist*, *A Tale of Two Cities*, *David Copperfield*, *A Christmas Carol*, *Hard Times*, *Great Expectations* and *The Old Curiosity Shop*.

In this collection of short stories we focus on Detectives.

Contents

The Trial of William Tinkling

WRITTEN BY HIMSELF AT THE AGE OF 8 YEARS

FOREWORD

The story contained herein was written by Charles Dickens in 1867. It is the first of four stories entitled "Holiday Romance" and was published originally in a children's magazine in America. It purports to be written by a child aged eight. It was republished in England in "All the Year Round" in 1868. For this and four other Christmas pieces Dickens received L1,000.

"Holiday Romance" was published in book form by Messrs Chapman & Hall in 1874, with "Edwin Drood" and other stories.

For this reprint the text of the story as it appeared in "All the Year Round" has been followed.

THE TRIAL OF WILLIAM TINKLING

This beginning-part is not made out of anybody's head, you know. It's real. You must believe this beginning-part more than what comes after, else you won't understand how what comes after came to be written. You must believe it all, but you must believe this most, please. I am the Editor of it. Bob Redforth (he's my cousin, and shaking the table on purpose) wanted to be the Editor of it, but I said he shouldn't because he couldn't. He has no idea of being an editor.

Nettie Ashford is my Bride. We were married in the right-hand closet in the corner of the dancing-school where first we met, with a ring (a green one) from Wilkingwater's toy-shop. I owed for it out of my pocket-money. When the rapturous ceremony was over, we all four went up the lane and let off a cannon (brought loaded in Bob Redforth's waistcoat-pocket) to announce our nuptials. It flew right up when it went off, and turned over. Next day, Lieutenant-Colonel Robin Redforth was united, with similar ceremonies, to Alice Rainbird. This time the cannon bust with a most terrific explosion, and made a puppy bark.

My peerless Bride was, at the period of which we now treat, in captivity at Miss Grimmer's. Drowvey and Grimmer is the partnership, and opinion is divided which is the greatest Beast. The lovely bride of the Colonel was also immured in the Dungeons of the same establishment. A vow was entered into between the Colonel and myself that we would cut them out on the following Wednesday, when walking two and two.

Under the desperate circumstances of the case, the active brain of the Colonel, combining with his lawless pursuit (he is a Pirate), suggested an attack with fireworks. This however, from motives of humanity, was abandoned as too expensive.

Lightly armed with a paper-knife buttoned up under his jacket, and waving the dreaded black flag at the end of a cane, the Colonel took command of me at 2 P.M. on the eventful and appointed day. He had drawn out the plan of attack on a piece of paper which was rolled up round a hoop-stick. He showed it to me. My position and my full-length portrait (but my real ears don't stick out horizontal) was behind a corner-lamp-post, with written orders to remain there till I should see Miss Drowvey fall. The Drowvey who was to fall was the one in spectacles, not the one with the large lavender bonnet. At that signal I was to rush forth, seize my Bride, and fight my way to the lane. There, a junction would be effected between myself and the Colonel; and putting our Brides behind us, between ourselves and the palings, we were to conquer or die.

The enemy appeared, approached. Waving his black flag, the Colonel attacked. Confusion ensued. Anxiously I awaited my signal, but my signal came not. So far from falling, the hated Drowvey in spectacles appeared to me to have muffled the Colonel's head in his outlawed banner, and to be pitching into him with a parasol. The one in the lavender bonnet also performed prodigies of valour with her fists on his back. Seeing that all was for the moment lost, I fought my desperate way hand to hand to the lane. Through taking the back road, I was so fortunate as to meet nobody, and arrived there uninterrupted.

It seemed an age, ere the Colonel joined me. He had been to the jobbing-tailor's to be sewn up in several places, and attributed our defeat to the refusal of the detested Drowvey to fall. Finding her so obstinate he had said to her in a loud voice, "Die, recreant!" but had found her no more open to reason on that point than the other.

My blooming Bride appeared, accompanied by the Colonel's Bride, at the Dancing-School next day. What? Was her face averted from me? Hah! Even so. With a look of scorn she put into my hand a bit of paper, and took another partner. On the paper was pencilled, "Heavens! Can I write the word! Is my husband a Cow?"

In the first bewilderment of my heated brain I tried to think what slanderer could have traced my family to the ignoble animal mentioned above. Vain were my endeavours. At the end of that dance I whispered the Colonel to come into the cloak-room, and I showed him the note.

"There is a syllable wanting," said he, with a gloomy brow.

"Hah! What syllable?" was my inquiry.

"She asks, Can she write the word? And no; you see she couldn't," said the Colonel, pointing out the passage.

"And the word was?" said I.

"Cow, cow, coward," hissed the Pirate-Colonel in my ear, and gave me back the note.

Feeling that I must for ever tread the earth a branded boy, person I mean, or that I must clear up my honour, I demanded to be tried by a Court-Martial. The Colonel admitted my right to be tried. Some difficulty was found in composing the court, on account of the Emperor of France's aunt refusing to let him come out. He was to be the President. 'Ere yet we had appointed a substitute, he made his escape over the back wall, and stood among us, a free monarch.

The court was held on the grass by the pond. I recognised in a certain Admiral among my judges my deadliest foe. A cocoa-nut had given rise to language that I could not brook. But confiding in my innocence, and also in the knowledge that the President of the United States (who sat next him) owed me a knife, I braced myself for the ordeal.

It was a solemn spectacle, that court. Two executioners with pinafores reversed, led me in. Under the shade of an umbrella, I perceived my Bride, supported by the Bride of the Pirate-Colonel. The President (having reproved a little female ensign for tittering, on a matter of Life or Death) called upon me to plead, "Coward or no Coward, Guilty or not Guilty?" I pleaded in a firm tone, "No Coward and Not Guilty." (The little female ensign being again reproved by the President for misconduct, mutinied, left the court, and threw stones.)

My implacable enemy, the Admiral, conducted the case against me. The Colonel's Bride was called to prove that I had remained behind the corner-lamp-post during the engagement. I might have been spared the anguish of my own Bride's being also made a witness to the same point, but the Admiral knew where to wound me. Be still my soul, no matter. The Colonel was then brought forward with his evidence.

It was for this point that I had saved myself up, as the turning-point of my case. Shaking myself free of my guards, who had no business to hold me, the stupids!

unless I was found guilty. I asked the Colonel what he considered the first duty of a soldier? 'Ere he could reply, the President of the United States rose and informed the court that my foe the Admiral had suggested "Bravery," and that prompting a witness wasn't fair. The President of the Court immediately ordered the Admiral's mouth to be filled with leaves, and tied up with string. I had the satisfaction of seeing the sentence carried into effect, before the proceedings went further.

I then took a paper from my trousers-pocket, and asked: "What do you consider, Colonel Redforth, the first duty of a soldier? Is it obedience?"

"It is," said the Colonel.

"Is that paper, please to look at it, in your hand?"

"It is," said the Colonel.

"Is it a military sketch?"

"It is," said the Colonel.

"Of an engagement?"

"Quite so," said the Colonel.

"Of the late engagement?"

"Of the late engagement."

"Please to describe it, and then hand it to the President of the Court."

From that triumphant moment my sufferings and my dangers were at an end. The court rose up and jumped, on discovering that I had strictly obeyed orders. My foe, the Admiral, who though muzzled was malignant yet, contrived to suggest that I was dishonoured by having quitted the field. But the Colonel himself had done as much, and gave his opinion, upon his word and honour as a Pirate, that when all was lost the field might be quitted without disgrace. I was going to be found "No Coward and Not Guilty," and my blooming Bride was going to be publicly restored to my arms in a procession, when an unlooked-for event disturbed the general rejoicing. This was no other than the Emperor of France's aunt catching hold of his hair. The proceedings abruptly terminated, and the court tumultuously dissolved.

It was when the shades of the next evening but one were beginning to fall, 'ere yet the silver beams of Luna touched the earth, that four forms might have been descried slowly advancing towards the weeping willow on the borders of the pond, the now deserted scene of the day before yesterday's agonies and triumphs. On a nearer approach, and by a practised eye, these might have been identified as the forms of the Pirate-Colonel with his Bride, and of the day before yesterday's gallant prisoner with his Bride.

On the beauteous faces of the Nymphs, dejection sat enthroned. All four reclined under the willow for some minutes without speaking, till at length the bride of the

Colonel poutingly observed, "It's of no use pretending any more, and we had better give it up."

"Hah!" exclaimed the Pirate. "Pretending?"

"Don't go on like that; you worry me," returned his Bride.

The lovely Bride of Tinkling echoed the incredible declaration. The two warriors exchanged stoney glances.

"If," said the Bride of the Pirate-Colonel, "grown-up people WON'T do what they ought to do, and WILL put us out, what comes of our pretending?"

"We only get into scrapes," said the Bride of Tinkling.

"You know very well," pursued the Colonel's Bride, "that Miss Drowvey wouldn't fall. You complained of it yourself. And you know how disgracefully the court-martial ended. As to our marriage; would my people acknowledge it at home?"

"Or would my people acknowledge ours?" said the Bride of Tinkling.

Again the two warriors exchanged stoney glances.

"If you knocked at the door and claimed me, after you were told to go away," said the Colonel's Bride, "you would only have your hair pulled, or your ears, or your nose."

"If you persisted in ringing at the bell and claiming Me," said the Bride of Tinkling to that gentleman, "you would have things dropped on your head from the window over the handle, or you would be played upon by the garden-engine."

"And at your own homes," resumed the Bride of the Colonel, "it would be just as bad. You would be sent to bed, or something equally undignified. Again: how would you support us?"

The Pirate-Colonel replied, in a courageous voice, "By rapine!" But his Bride retorted, suppose the grown-up people wouldn't be rapined? Then, said the Colonel, they should pay the penalty in Blood. But suppose they should object, retorted his bride, and wouldn't pay the penalty in Blood or anything else?

A mournful silence ensued.

"Then do you no longer love me, Alice?" asked the Colonel.

"Redforth! I am ever thine," returned his Bride.

"Then do you no longer love me, Nettie?" asked the present writer.

"Tinkling! I am ever thine," returned my Bride.

We all four embraced. Let me not be misunderstood by the giddy. The Colonel embraced his own Bride, and I embraced mine. But two times two make four.

"Nettie and I," said Alice, mournfully, "have been considering our position. The grown-up people are too strong for us. They make us ridiculous. Besides, they have changed the times. William Tinkling's baby-brother was christened yesterday. What took place? Was any king present? Answer, William."

I said No, unless disguised as great-uncle Chopper.

"Any queen?"

There had been no queen that I knew of at our house. There might have been one in the kitchen; but I didn't think so, or the servants would have mentioned it.

"Any fairies?"

None that were visible.

"We had an idea among us, I think," said Alice, with a melancholy smile, "we four, that Miss Grimmer would prove to be the wicked fairy, and would come in at the christening with her crutch-stick, and give the child a bad gift? Was there anything of that sort? Answer, William."

I said that Ma had said afterwards (and so she had), that great-uncle Chopper's gift was a shabby one; but she hadn't said a bad one. She had called it shabby, electrotyped, second-hand, and below his income.

"It must be the grown-up people who have changed all this," said Alice. "We couldn't have changed it, if we had been so inclined, and we never should have been. Or perhaps Miss Grimmer is a wicked fairy, after all, and won't act up to it, because the grown-up people have persuaded her not to. Either way, they would make us ridiculous if we told them what we expected."

"Tyrants!" muttered the Pirate-Colonel.

"Nay, my Redforth," said Alice, "say not so. Call not names, my Redforth, or they will apply to Pa."

"Let 'em," said the Colonel. "I don't care. Who's he?"

Tinkling here undertook the perilous task of remonstrating with his lawless friend, who consented to withdraw the moody expressions above quoted.

"What remains for us to do?" Alice went on in her mild wise way. "We must educate, we must pretend in a new manner, we must wait."

The Colonel clenched his teeth, four out in front, and a piece off another, and he had been twice dragged to the door of a dentist-despot, but had escaped from his guards. "How educate? How pretend in a new manner? How wait?"

"Educate the grown-up people," replied Alice. "We part to-night. Yes, Redforth," for the Colonel tucked up his cuffs, "part to-night! Let us in these next Holidays, now going to begin, throw our thoughts into something educational for the grown-up people, hinting to them how things ought to be. Let us veil our meaning under a mask of romance;[A] you, I, and Nettie. William Tinkling being the plainest and quickest writer, shall copy out. Is it agreed?"

The Colonel answered, sulkily, "I don't mind." He then asked, "How about pretending?"

"We will pretend," said Alice, "that we are children; not that we are those grown-up people who won't help us out as they ought, and who understand us so badly."

The Colonel, still much dissatisfied, growled, "How about waiting?"

"We will wait," answered little Alice, taking Nettie's hand in hers, and looking up to the sky, "we will wait, ever constant and true, till the times have got so changed as that everything helps us out, and nothing makes us ridiculous, and the fairies have come back. We will wait, ever constant and true, till we are eighty, ninety, or one hundred. And then the fairies will send us children, and we will help them out, poor pretty little creatures, if they pretend ever so much."

"So we will, dear," said Nettie Ashford, taking her round the waist with both arms and kissing her. "And now if my Husband will go and buy some cherries for us, I have got some money."

In the friendliest manner I invited the Colonel to go with me; but he so far forgot himself as to acknowledge the invitation by kicking out behind, and then lying down on his stomach on the grass, pulling it up and chewing it. When I came back, however, Alice had nearly brought him out of his vexation, and was soothing him by telling him how soon we should all be ninety.

As we sat under the willow-tree and ate the cherries (fair, for Alice shared them out), we played at being ninety. Nettie complained that she had a bone in her old back and it made her hobble, and Alice sang a song in an old woman's way, but it was very pretty, and we were all merry. At least I don't know about merry exactly, but all comfortable.

There was a most tremendous lot of cherries and Alice always had with her some neat little bag or box or case, to hold things. In it, that night, was a tiny wine-glass. So Alice and Nettie said they would make some cherry-wine to drink our love at parting.

Each of us had a glassful, and it was delicious, and each of us drank the toast, "Our love at parting." The Colonel drank his wine last, and it got into my head directly that it got into his directly. Anyhow his eyes rolled immediately after he had turned the glass upside down, and he took me on one side and proposed in a hoarse whisper that we should "Cut 'em out still."

"How did he mean?" I asked my lawless friend.

"Cut our Brides out," said the Colonel, "and then cut our way, without going down a single turning, Bang to the Spanish Main!"

We might have tried it, though I didn't think it would answer; only we looked round and saw that there was nothing but moonlight under the willow-tree, and that our pretty, pretty wives were gone. We burst out crying. The Colonel gave in second, and came to first; but he gave in strong.

We were ashamed of our red eyes, and hung about for half an hour to whiten them. Likewise a piece of chalk round the rims, I doing the Colonel's, and he mine, but afterwards found in the bedroom looking-glass not natural, besides inflammation. Our conversation turned on being ninety. The Colonel told me he had a pair of boots that wanted soleing and heeling but he thought it hardly worth while to mention it to his father, as he himself should so soon be ninety, when he thought shoes would be more convenient. The Colonel also told me with his hand upon his hip that he felt himself already getting on in life, and turning rheumatic. And I told him the same. And when they said at our house at supper (they are always bothering about something) that I stooped, I felt so glad!

This is the end of the beginning-part that you were to believe most.

[Footnote A: The titles of the romances by which Alice Rainbird, Nettie Ashford and the Pirate-Colonel sought to veil their meanings will be found on page 31.]

Three Detective Anecdotes

I. THE PAIR OF GLOVES

'It's a singler story, sir,' said Inspector Wield, of the Detective Police, who, in company with Sergeants Dornton and Mith, paid us another twilight visit, one July evening; 'and I've been thinking you might like to know it.

'It's concerning the murder of the young woman, Eliza Grimwood, some years ago, over in the Waterloo Road. She was commonly called The Countess, because of her handsome appearance and her proud way of carrying of herself; and when I saw the poor Countess (I had known her well to speak to), lying dead, with her throat cut, on the floor of her bedroom, you'll believe me that a variety of reflections calculated to make a man rather low in his spirits, came into my head.

'That's neither here nor there. I went to the house the morning after the murder, and examined the body, and made a general observation of the bedroom where it was. Turning down the pillow of the bed with my hand, I found, underneath it, a pair of gloves. A pair of gentleman's dress gloves, very dirty; and inside the lining, the letters TR, and a cross.

'Well, sir, I took them gloves away, and I showed 'em to the magistrate, over at Union Hall, before whom the case was. He says, "Wield," he says, "there's no doubt this is a discovery that may lead to something very important; and what you have got to do, Wield, is, to find out the owner of these gloves."

'I was of the same opinion, of course, and I went at it immediately. I looked at the gloves pretty narrowly, and it was my opinion that they had been cleaned. There was a smell of sulphur and rosin about 'em, you know, which cleaned gloves usually have, more or less. I took 'em over to a friend of mine at Kennington, who was in that line, and I put it to him. "What do you say now? Have these gloves been cleaned?" "These gloves have been cleaned," says he. "Have you any idea who cleaned them?" says I. "Not at all," says he; "I've a very distinct idea who DIDN'T clean 'em, and that's myself. But I'll tell you what, Wield, there ain't above eight or nine reg'lar glove-cleaners in London," - there were not, at that time, it seems - "and I think I can give you their addresses, and you may find out, by that means, who did clean 'em." Accordingly, he gave me the directions, and I went here, and I went there, and I looked up this man, and I looked up that man; but, though they all agreed that the gloves had been cleaned, I couldn't find the man, woman, or child, that had cleaned that aforesaid pair of gloves.

'What with this person not being at home, and that person being expected home in the afternoon, and so forth, the inquiry took me three days. On the evening of the third day, coming over Waterloo Bridge from the Surrey side of the river, quite beat, and very much vexed and disappointed, I thought I'd have a shilling's worth of entertainment at the Lyceum Theatre to freshen myself up. So I went into the Pit, at half-price, and I sat myself down next to a very quiet, modest sort of young man. Seeing I was a stranger (which I thought it just as well to appear to be) he told me the names of the actors on the stage, and we got into conversation. When the play was over, we came out together, and I said, "We've been very companionable and agreeable, and perhaps you wouldn't object to a drain?" "Well, you're very good," says he; "I SHOULDN'T object to a drain." Accordingly, we went to a public- house, near the Theatre, sat ourselves down in a quiet room up- stairs on the first floor, and called for a pint of half-and-half, apiece, and a pipe.

'Well, sir, we put our pipes aboard, and we drank our half-and- half, and sat a-talking, very sociably, when the young man says, "You must excuse me stopping very long," he says, "because I'm forced to go home in good time. I must be at work all night." "At work all night?" says I. "You ain't a baker?" "No," he says, laughing, "I ain't a baker." "I thought not," says I, "you haven't the looks of a baker." "No," says he, "I'm a glove-cleaner."

'I never was more astonished in my life, than when I heard them words come out of his lips. "You're a glove-cleaner, are you?" says I. "Yes," he says, "I am." "Then, perhaps," says I, taking the gloves out of my pocket, "you can tell me who cleaned this pair of gloves? It's a rum story," I says. "I was dining over at Lambeth, the other day, at a free-and-easy - quite promiscuous - with a public company - when some gentleman, he left these gloves behind him! Another gentleman and me, you see, we laid a wager of a sovereign, that I wouldn't find out who they belonged to. I've spent as much as seven shillings already, in trying to discover; but, if you could help me, I'd stand another seven and welcome. You see there's TR and a cross, inside." "I see," he says. "Bless you, I know these gloves very well! I've seen dozens of pairs belonging to the same party." "No?" says I. "Yes," says he. "Then you know who cleaned 'em?" says I. "Rather so," says he. "My father cleaned 'em."

'"Where does your father live?" says I. "Just round the corner," says the young man, "near Exeter Street, here. He'll tell you who they belong to, directly." "Would you come round with me now?" says I. "Certainly," says he, "but you needn't tell my father that you found me at the play, you know, because he mightn't like it." "All right!" We went round to the place, and there we found an old man in a white apron, with two or three daughters, all rubbing and cleaning away at lots of gloves, in a front parlour. "Oh, Father!" says the young man, "here's a person been and made a bet about the ownership of a pair of gloves, and I've told him you can settle it." "Good evening, sir," says I to the old gentleman. "Here's the gloves your son speaks of. Letters TR, you see, and a cross." "Oh yes," he says, "I know these gloves very well; I've cleaned dozens of pairs of 'em. They belong to Mr. Trinkle, the great upholsterer in Cheapside." "Did you get 'em from Mr. Trinkle, direct," says I, "if you'll excuse my asking the question?" "No," says he; "Mr. Trinkle always sends 'em to Mr. Phibbs's, the haberdasher's, opposite his shop, and the haberdasher sends 'em to me." "Perhaps YOU wouldn't object to a drain?" says I. "Not in the least!" says he. So I took the old gentleman out, and had a little more talk with him and his son, over a glass, and we parted excellent friends.

'This was late on a Saturday night. First thing on the Monday morning, I went to the haberdasher's shop, opposite Mr. Trinkle's, the great upholsterer's in Cheapside. "Mr. Phibbs in the way?" "My name is Phibbs." "Oh! I believe you sent this pair of gloves to be cleaned?" "Yes, I did, for young Mr. Trinkle over the way. There he is in the shop!" "Oh! that's him in the shop, is it? Him in the green coat?" "The same individual." "Well, Mr. Phibbs, this is an unpleasant affair; but the fact is, I am Inspector Wield of the Detective Police, and I found these gloves under the pillow of the young woman that was murdered the other day, over in the Waterloo Road!" "Good Heaven!" says he. "He's a most respectable young man, and if his father was to hear of it, it would be the ruin of him!" "I'm very sorry for it," says I, "but I must take him into custody." "Good Heaven!" says Mr. Phibbs, again; "can nothing be done?" "Nothing," says I. "Will you allow me to call him over here," says he, "that his father may not see it done?" "I don't object to that," says I; "but unfortunately, Mr. Phibbs, I can't allow of any communication between you. If any was attempted, I should have to interfere directly. Perhaps you'll beckon him over here?' Mr. Phibbs went to the door and beckoned, and the young fellow came across the street directly; a smart, brisk young fellow.

'"Good morning, sir," says I. "Good morning, sir," says he. "Would you allow me to inquire, sir," says I, "if you ever had any acquaintance with a party of the name of Grimwood?" "Grimwood! Grimwood!" says he. "No!" "You know the Waterloo Road?" "Oh! of course I know the Waterloo Road!" "Happen to have heard of a young woman being murdered there?" "Yes, I read it in the paper, and very sorry I was to read it." "Here's a pair of gloves belonging to you, that I found under her pillow the morning afterwards!"

'He was in a dreadful state, sir; a dreadful state I "Mr. Wield," he says, "upon my solemn oath I never was there. I never so much as saw her, to my knowledge, in my life!" "I am very sorry," says I. "To tell you the truth; I don't think you ARE the murderer, but I must take you to Union Hall in a cab. However, I think it's a case of that sort, that, at present, at all events, the magistrate will hear it in private."

*

'A private examination took place, and then it came out that this young man was acquainted with a cousin of the unfortunate Eliza Grimwood, and that, calling to see this cousin a day or two before the murder, he left these gloves upon the table. Who should come in, shortly afterwards, but Eliza Grimwood! "Whose gloves are these?" she says, taking 'em up. "Those are Mr. Trinkle's gloves," says her cousin. "Oh!" says she, "they are very dirty, and of no use to him, I am sure. I shall take 'em away for my girl to clean the stoves with." And she put 'em in her pocket. The girl had used 'em to clean the stoves, and, I have no doubt, had left 'em lying on the bedroom mantelpiece, or on the drawers, or somewhere; and her mistress, looking round to see that the room was tidy, had caught 'em up and put 'em under the pillow where I found 'em.

That's the story, sir.'

II. THE ARTFUL TOUCH

'One of the most BEAUTIFUL things that ever was done, perhaps,' said Inspector Wield, emphasising the adjective, as preparing us to expect dexterity or ingenuity rather than strong interest, 'was a move of Sergeant Witchem's. It was a lovely idea!

'Witchem and me were down at Epsom one Derby Day, waiting at the station for the Swell Mob. As I mentioned, when we were talking about these things before, we are ready at the station when there's races, or an Agricultural Show, or a Chancellor sworn in for an university, or Jenny Lind, or anything of that sort; and as the Swell Mob come down, we send 'em back again by the next train. But some of the Swell Mob, on the occasion of this Derby that I refer to, so far kidded us as to hire a horse and shay; start away from London by Whitechapel, and miles round; come into Epsom from the opposite direction; and go to work, right and left, on the course, while we were waiting for 'em at the Rail. That, however, ain't the point of what I'm going to tell you.

'While Witchem and me were waiting at the station, there comes up one Mr. Tatt; a gentleman formerly in the public line, quite an amateur Detective in his way, and very much respected. "Halloa, Charley Wield," he says. "What are you doing here? On the look out for some of your old friends?" "Yes, the old move, Mr. Tatt." "Come along," he says, "you and Witchem, and have a glass of sherry." "We can't stir from the place," says I, "till the next train comes in; but after that, we will with pleasure." Mr. Tatt waits, and the train comes in, and then Witchem and me go off with him to the Hotel. Mr. Tatt he's got up quite regardless of expense, for the occasion; and in his shirt-front there's a beautiful diamond prop, cost him fifteen or twenty pound - a very handsome pin indeed. We drink our sherry at the bar, and have had our three or four glasses, when Witchem cries suddenly, "Look out, Mr. Wield! stand fast!" and a dash is made into the place by the Swell Mob - four of 'em - that have come down as I tell you, and in a moment Mr. Tatt's prop is gone! Witchem, he cuts 'em off at the door, I lay about me as hard as I can, Mr. Tatt shows fight like a good 'un, and there we are, all down together, heads and heels, knocking about on the floor of the bar - perhaps you never see such a scene of confusion! However, we stick to our men (Mr. Tatt being as good as any officer), and we take 'em all, and carry 'em off to the station.' The station's full of people, who have been took on the course; and it's a precious piece of work to get 'em secured. However, we do it at last, and we search 'em; but nothing's found upon 'em, and they're locked up; and a pretty state of heat we are in by that time, I assure you!

'I was very blank over it, myself, to think that the prop had been passed away; and I said to Witchem, when we had set 'em to rights, and were cooling ourselves along with Mr. Tatt, "we don't take much by THIS move, anyway, for nothing's found upon 'em, and it's only the braggadocia, (1) after all." "What do you mean, Mr. Wield?" says Witchem. "Here's the diamond pin!" and in the palm of his hand there it was, safe and sound! "Why, in the name of wonder," says me and Mr. Tatt, in astonishment, "how did you come by that?" "I'll tell you how I come by it," says he. "I saw which of 'em took it; and when we were all down on the floor together, knocking about, I just gave him a little touch on the back of his hand, as I knew his pal would; and he thought it WAS his pal; and gave it me!" It was beautiful, beau-ti-ful!

'Even that was hardly the best of the case, for that chap was tried at the Quarter Sessions at Guildford. You know what Quarter Sessions are, sir. Well, if you'll believe me, while them slow justices were looking over the Acts of Parliament, to see what they could do to him, I'm blowed if he didn't cut out of the dock before their faces! He cut out of the dock, sir, then and there; swam across a river; and got up into a tree to dry himself. In the tree he was took - an old woman having seen him climb up - and Witchem's artful touch transported him!'

III. THE SOFA

"What young men will do, sometimes, to ruin themselves and break their friends' hearts,' said Sergeant Dornton, 'it's surprising! I had a case at Saint Blank's Hospital which was of this sort. A bad case, indeed, with a bad end!

'The Secretary, and the House-Surgeon, and the Treasurer, of Saint Blank's Hospital, came to Scotland Yard to give information of numerous robberies having been committed on the students. The students could leave nothing in the pockets of their great-coats, while the great-coats were hanging at the hospital, but it was almost certain to be stolen. Property of various descriptions was constantly being lost; and the gentlemen were naturally uneasy about it, and anxious, for the credit of the institution, that the thief or thieves should be discovered. The case was entrusted to me, and I went to the hospital.

'"Now, gentlemen," said I, after we had talked it over; "I understand this property is usually lost from one room."

'Yes, they said. It was.

'"I should wish, if you please," said I, "to see the room."

'It was a good-sized bare room down-stairs, with a few tables and forms in it, and a row of pegs, all round, for hats and coats.

'"Next, gentlemen," said I, "do you suspect anybody?"

'Yes, they said. They did suspect somebody. They were sorry to say, they suspected one of the porters.

'"I should like," said I, "to have that man pointed out to me, and to have a little time to look after him."

'He was pointed out, and I looked after him, and then I went back to the hospital, and said, "Now, gentlemen, it's not the porter. He's, unfortunately for himself, a little too fond of drink, but he's nothing worse. My suspicion is, that these robberies are committed by one of the students; and if you'll put me a sofa into that room where the pegs are - as there's no closet - I think I shall be able to detect the thief. I wish the sofa, if you please, to be covered with chintz, or something of that sort, so that I may lie on my chest, underneath it, without being seen."

'The sofa was provided, and next day at eleven o'clock, before any of the students came, I went there, with those gentlemen, to get underneath it. It turned out to be one of those old-fashioned sofas with a great cross-beam at the bottom, that would have broken my back in no time if I could ever have got below it. We had quite a job to break all this away in the time; however, I fell to work, and they fell to work, and we broke it out, and made a clear place for me. I got under the sofa, lay down on my chest, took out my knife, and made a convenient hole in the chintz to look through. It was then settled between me and the gentlemen that when the students were all up in the wards, one of the gentlemen should come in, and hang up a great-coat on one of the pegs. And that that great-coat should have, in one of the pockets, a pocket-book containing marked money.

'After I had been there some time, the students began to drop into the room, by ones, and twos, and threes, and to talk about all sorts of things, little thinking there was anybody under the sofa - and then to go up-stairs. At last there came in one who remained until he was alone in the room by himself. A tallish, good-looking young man of one or two and twenty, with a light whisker. He went to a particular hat-peg, took off a good hat that was hanging there, tried it on, hung his own hat in its place, and hung that hat on another peg, nearly opposite to me. I then felt quite certain that he was the thief, and would come back by-and-by.

'When they were all up-stairs, the gentleman came in with the great-coat. I showed him where to hang it, so that I might have a good view of it; and he went away; and I lay under the sofa on my chest, for a couple of hours or so, waiting.

'At last, the same young man came down. He walked across the room, whistling - stopped and listened - took another walk and whistled - stopped again, and listened - then began to go regularly round the pegs, feeling in the pockets of all the coats. When he came to the great-coat, and felt the pocket-book, he was so eager and so hurried that he broke the strap in tearing it open. As he began to put the money in his pocket, I crawled out from under the sofa, and his eyes met mine.

'My face, as you may perceive, is brown now, but it was pale at that time, my health not being good; and looked as long as a horse's. Besides which, there was a great draught of air from the door, underneath the sofa, and I had tied a handkerchief round my head; so what I looked like, altogether, I don't know. He turned blue - literally blue - when he saw me crawling out, and I couldn't feel surprised at it.

'"I am an officer of the Detective Police," said I, "and have been lying here, since you first came in this morning. I regret, for the sake of yourself and your friends, that you should have done what you have; but this case is complete. You have the pocket-book in your hand and the money upon you; and I must take you into custody!"

'It was impossible to make out any case in his behalf, and on his trial he pleaded guilty. How or when he got the means I don't know; but while he was awaiting his sentence, he poisoned himself in Newgate.'

We inquired of this officer, on the conclusion of the foregoing anecdote, whether the time appeared long, or short, when he lay in that constrained position under the sofa?

'Why, you see, sir,' he replied, 'if he hadn't come in, the first time, and I had not been quite sure he was the thief, and would return, the time would have seemed long. But, as it was, I being dead certain of my man, the time seemed pretty short.'

Footnotes: *(1) Three months' imprisonment as reputed thieves.*

The Detective Police

We are not by any means devout believers in the old Bow Street Police. To say the truth, we think there was a vast amount of humbug about those worthies. Apart from many of them being men of very indifferent character, and far too much in the habit of consorting with thieves and the like, they never lost a public occasion of jobbing and trading in mystery and making the most of themselves. Continually puffed besides by incompetent magistrates anxious to conceal their own deficiencies, and hand-in-glove with the penny-a-liners of that time, they became a sort of superstition. Although as a Preventive Police they were utterly ineffective, and as a Detective Police were very loose and uncertain in their operations, they remain with some people a superstition to the present day.

On the other hand, the Detective Force organised since the establishment of the existing Police, is so well chosen and trained, proceeds so systematically and quietly, does its business in such a workmanlike manner, and is always so calmly and steadily engaged in the service of the public, that the public really do not know enough of it, to know a tithe of its usefulness. Impressed with this conviction, and interested in the men themselves, we represented to the authorities at Scotland Yard, that we should be glad, if there were no official objection, to have some talk with the Detectives. A most obliging and ready permission being given, a certain evening was appointed with a certain Inspector for a social conference between ourselves and the Detectives, at The Household Words Office in Wellington Street, Strand, London. In consequence of which appointment the party 'came off,' which we are about to describe. And we beg to repeat that, avoiding such topics as it might for obvious reasons be injurious to the public, or disagreeable to respectable individuals, to touch upon in print, our description is as exact as we can make it.

The reader will have the goodness to imagine the Sanctum Sanctorum of Household Words. Anything that best suits the reader's fancy, will best represent that magnificent chamber. We merely stipulate for a round table in the middle, with some glasses and cigars arranged upon it; and the editorial sofa elegantly hemmed in between that stately piece of furniture and the wall.

It is a sultry evening at dusk. The stones of Wellington Street are hot and gritty, and the watermen and hackney-coachmen at the Theatre opposite, are much flushed and aggravated. Carriages are constantly setting down the people who have come to Fairy-Land; and there is a mighty shouting and bellowing every now and then, deafening us for the moment, through the open windows.

Just at dusk, Inspectors Wield and Stalker are announced; but we do not undertake to warrant the orthography of any of the names here mentioned. Inspector Wield presents Inspector Stalker. Inspector Wield is a middle-aged man of a portly presence, with a large, moist, knowing eye, a husky voice, and a habit of emphasising his conversation by the aid of a corpulent fore-finger, which is constantly in juxtaposition with his eyes or nose. Inspector Stalker is a shrewd, hard-headed Scotchman - in appearance not at all unlike a very acute, thoroughly-trained schoolmaster, from the Normal Establishment at Glasgow. Inspector Wield one might have known, perhaps, for what he is - Inspector Stalker, never.

The ceremonies of reception over, Inspectors Wield and Stalker observe that they have brought some sergeants with them. The sergeants are presented - five in number, Sergeant Dornton, Sergeant Witchem, Sergeant Mith, Sergeant Fendall, and Sergeant Straw. We have the whole Detective Force from Scotland Yard, with one exception. They sit down in a semi-circle (the two Inspectors at the two ends) at a little distance from the round table, facing the editorial sofa. Every man of them, in a glance, immediately takes an inventory of the furniture and an accurate sketch of the editorial presence. The Editor feels that any gentleman in company could take him up, if need should be, without the smallest hesitation, twenty years hence.

The whole party are in plain clothes. Sergeant Dornton about fifty years of age, with a ruddy face and a high sunburnt forehead, has the air of one who has been a Sergeant in the army - he might have sat to Wilkie for the Soldier in the Reading of the Will. He is famous for steadily pursuing the inductive process, and, from small beginnings, working on from clue to clue until he bags his man. Sergeant Witchem, shorter and thicker-set, and marked with the small-pox, has something of a reserved and thoughtful air, as if he were engaged in deep arithmetical calculations. He is renowned for his acquaintance with the swell mob. Sergeant Mith, a smooth-faced man with a fresh bright complexion, and a strange air of simplicity, is a dab at housebreakers. Sergeant Fendall, a light- haired, well-spoken, polite person, is a prodigious hand at pursuing private inquiries of a delicate nature. Straw, a little wiry Sergeant of meek demeanour and strong sense, would knock at a door and ask a series of questions in any mild character you choose to prescribe to him, from a charity-boy upwards, and seem as innocent as an infant. They are, one and all, respectable-looking men; of perfectly good deportment and unusual intelligence; with nothing lounging or slinking in their manners; with an air of keen observation and quick perception when addressed; and generally presenting in their faces, traces more or less marked of habitually leading lives of strong mental excitement. They have all good eyes; and they all can, and they all do, look full at whomsoever they speak to.

We light the cigars, and hand round the glasses (which are very temperately used indeed), and the conversation begins by a modest amateur reference on the Editorial part to the swell mob. Inspector Wield immediately removes his cigar from his lips, waves his right hand, and says, 'Regarding the swell mob, sir, I can't do better than call upon Sergeant Witchem. Because the reason why? I'll tell you. Sergeant Witchem is better acquainted with the swell mob than any officer in London.'

Our heart leaping up when we beheld this rainbow in the sky, we turn to Sergeant Witchem, who very concisely, and in well-chosen language, goes into the subject forthwith. Meantime, the whole of his brother officers are closely interested in attending to what he says, and observing its effect. Presently they begin to strike in, one or two together, when an opportunity offers, and the conversation becomes general. But these brother officers only come in to the assistance of each other - not to the contradiction - and a more amicable brotherhood there could not be. From the swell mob, we diverge to the kindred topics of cracksmen, fences, public- house dancers, area-sneaks, designing young people who go out 'gonophing,' and other 'schools.' It is observable throughout these revelations, that Inspector Stalker, the Scotchman, is always exact and statistical, and that when any question of figures arises, everybody as by one consent pauses, and looks to him.

When we have exhausted the various schools of Art - during which discussion the whole body have remained profoundly attentive, except when some unusual noise at the Theatre over the way has induced some gentleman to glance inquiringly towards the window in that direction, behind his next neighbour's back - we burrow for information on such points as the following. Whether there really are any highway robberies in London, or whether some circumstances not convenient to be mentioned by the aggrieved party, usually precede the robberies complained of, under that head, which quite change their character? Certainly the latter, almost always. Whether in the case of robberies in houses, where servants are necessarily exposed to doubt, innocence under suspicion ever becomes so like guilt in appearance, that a good officer need be cautious how he judges it? Undoubtedly. Nothing is so common or deceptive as such appearances at first. Whether in a place of public amusement, a thief knows an officer, and an officer knows a thief - supposing them, beforehand, strangers to each other - because each recognises in the other, under all disguise, an inattention to what is going on, and a purpose that is not the purpose of being entertained? Yes. That's the way exactly. Whether it is reasonable or ridiculous to trust to the alleged experiences of thieves as narrated by themselves, in prisons, or penitentiaries, or anywhere? In general, nothing more absurd. Lying is their habit and their trade; and they would rather lie - even if they hadn't an interest in it, and didn't want to make themselves agreeable - than tell the truth.

From these topics, we glide into a review of the most celebrated and horrible of the great crimes that have been committed within the last fifteen or twenty years. The men engaged in the discovery of almost all of them, and in the pursuit or apprehension of the murderers, are here, down to the very last instance. One of our guests gave chase to and boarded the emigrant ship, in which the murderess last hanged in London was supposed to have embarked. We learn from him that his errand was not announced to the passengers, who may have no idea of it to this hour. That he went below, with the captain, lamp in hand - it being dark, and the whole steerage abed and sea-sick - and engaged the Mrs. Manning who WAS on board, in a conversation about her luggage, until she was, with no small pains, induced to raise her head, and turn her face towards the light. Satisfied that she was not the object of his search, he quietly re-embarked in the Government steamer along-side, and steamed home again with the intelligence.

When we have exhausted these subjects, too, which occupy a considerable time in the discussion, two or three leave their chairs, whisper Sergeant Witchem, and resume their seat. Sergeant Witchem, leaning forward a little, and placing a hand on each of his legs, then modestly speaks as follows:

'My brother-officers wish me to relate a little account of my taking Tally-ho Thompson. A man oughtn't to tell what he has done himself; but still, as nobody was with me, and, consequently, as nobody but myself can tell it, I'll do it in the best way I can, if it should meet your approval.'

We assure Sergeant Witchem that he will oblige us very much, and we all compose ourselves to listen with great interest and attention.

'Tally-ho Thompson,' says Sergeant Witchem, after merely wetting his lips with his brandy-and-water, 'Tally-ho Thompson was a famous horse-stealer, couper, and magsman. Thompson, in conjunction with a pal that occasionally worked with him, gammoned a countryman out of a good round sum of money, under pretence of getting him a situation - the regular old dodge - and was afterwards in the "Hue and Cry" for a horse - a horse that he stole down in Hertfordshire. I had to look after Thompson, and I applied myself, of course, in the first instance, to discovering where he was. Now, Thompson's wife lived, along with a little daughter, at Chelsea. Knowing that Thompson was somewhere in the country, I watched the house - especially at post-time in the morning - thinking Thompson was pretty likely to write to her. Sure enough, one morning the postman comes up, and delivers a letter at Mrs. Thompson's door. Little girl opens the door, and takes it in. We're not always sure of postmen, though the people at the post-offices are always very obliging. A postman may help us, or he may not, - just as it happens. However, I go across the road, and I say to the postman, after he has left the letter, "Good morning! how are you?" "How are YOU!" says he. "You've just delivered a letter for Mrs. Thompson." "Yes, I have." "You didn't happen to remark what the post-mark was, perhaps?" "No," says he, "I didn't." "Come," says I, "I'll be plain with you. I'm in a small way of business, and I have given Thompson credit, and I can't afford to lose what he owes me. I know he's got money, and I know he's in the country, and if you could tell me what the post-mark was, I should be very much obliged to you, and you'd do a service to a tradesman in a small way of business that can't afford a loss." "Well," he said, "I do assure you that I did not observe what the post-mark was; all I know is, that there was money in the letter - I should say a sovereign." This was enough for me, because of course I knew that Thompson having sent his wife money, it was probable she'd write to Thompson, by return of post, to acknowledge the receipt. So I said "Thankee" to the postman, and I kept on the watch. In the afternoon I saw the little girl come out. Of course I followed her. She went into a stationer's shop, and I needn't say to you that I looked in at the window. She bought some writing-paper and envelopes, and a pen. I think to myself, "That'll do!" - watch her home again - and don't go away, you may be sure, knowing that Mrs. Thompson was writing her letter to Tally-ho, and that the letter would be posted presently. In about an hour or so, out came the little girl again, with the letter in her hand. I went up, and said something to the child, whatever it might have been; but I couldn't see the direction of the letter, because she held it with the seal upwards. However, I observed that on the back of the letter there was what we call a kiss - a drop of wax by the side of the seal - and again, you understand, that was enough for me. I saw her post the letter, waited till she was gone, then went into the shop, and asked to see the Master. When he came out, I told him, "Now, I'm an Officer in the Detective Force; there's a letter with a kiss been posted here just now, for a man that I'm in search of; and what I have to ask of you, is, that you will let me look at the direction of that letter." He was very civil - took a lot of letters from the box in the window - shook 'em out on the counter with the faces downwards - and there among 'em was the identical letter with the kiss. It was directed, Mr. Thomas Pigeon, Post Office, B-, to be left till called for. Down I went to B- (a hundred and twenty miles or so) that night. Early next morning I went to the Post Office; saw the gentleman in charge of that department; told him who I was; and that my object was to see, and track, the party that should come for the letter for Mr. Thomas Pigeon. He was very polite, and said, "You shall have every assistance we can give you; you can wait inside the office; and we'll take care to let you know when anybody comes for the letter." Well, I waited there three days, and began to think that nobody ever WOULD come. At last the clerk whispered to me, "Here! Detective! Somebody's come for the letter!" "Keep him a minute," said I, and I ran round to the outside of the office. There I saw a young chap with the appearance of an Ostler, holding a horse by the bridle - stretching the bridle across the pavement, while he waited at the Post Office Window for the letter. I began to pat the horse, and that; and I said to the boy, "Why, this is Mr. Jones's Mare!" "No. It an't." "No?" said I. "She's very like Mr. Jones's Mare!" "She an't Mr. Jones's Mare, anyhow," says he. "It's Mr. So and So's, of the Warwick Arms." And up he jumped, and off he went - letter and all. I got a cab, followed on the box, and was so quick after him that I came into the stable-yard of the Warwick Arms, by one gate, just as he came in by another. I went into the bar, where there was a young woman serving, and called for a glass of brandy-and-water. He came in directly, and handed her the letter. She casually looked at it, without saying anything, and stuck it up behind the glass over the chimney-piece. What was to be done next?

'I turned it over in my mind while I drank my brandy-and-water (looking pretty sharp at the letter the while), but I couldn't see my way out of it at all. I tried to get lodgings in the house, but there had been a horse-fair, or something of that sort, and it was full. I was obliged to put up somewhere else, but I came backwards and forwards to the bar for a couple of days, and there was the letter always behind the glass. At last I thought I'd write a letter to Mr. Pigeon myself, and see what that would do. So I wrote one, and posted it, but I purposely addressed it, Mr. John Pigeon, instead of Mr. Thomas Pigeon, to see what THAT would do. In the morning (a very wet morning it was) I watched the postman down the street, and cut into the bar, just before he reached the Warwick Arms. In he came presently with my letter. "Is there a Mr. John Pigeon staying here?" "No! - stop a bit though," says the barmaid; and she took down the letter behind the glass. "No," says she, "it's Thomas, and HE is not staying here. Would you do me a favour, and post this for me, as it is so wet?" The postman said Yes; she folded it in another envelope, directed it, and gave it him. He put it in his hat, and away he went.

'I had no difficulty in finding out the direction of that letter. It was addressed Mr. Thomas Pigeon, Post Office, R-, Northamptonshire, to be left till called for. Off I started directly for R-; I said the same at the Post Office there, as I had said at B-; and again I waited three days before anybody came. At last another chap on horseback came. "Any letters for Mr. Thomas Pigeon?" "Where do you come from?" "New Inn, near R-." He got the letter, and away HE went at a canter.

'I made my inquiries about the New Inn, near R-, and hearing it was a solitary sort of house, a little in the horse line, about a couple of miles from the station, I thought I'd go and have a look at it. I found it what it had been described, and sauntered in, to look about me. The landlady was in the bar, and I was trying to get into conversation with her; asked her how business was, and spoke about the wet weather, and so on; when I saw, through an open door, three men sitting by the fire in a sort of parlour, or kitchen; and one of those men, according to the description I had of him, was Tally-ho Thompson!

'I went and sat down among 'em, and tried to make things agreeable; but they were very shy - wouldn't talk at all - looked at me, and at one another, in a way quite the reverse of sociable. I reckoned 'em up, and finding that they were all three bigger men than me, and considering that their looks were ugly - that it was a lonely place - railroad station two miles off - and night coming on - thought I couldn't do better than have a drop of brandy-and-water to keep my courage up. So I called for my brandy-and-water; and as I was sitting drinking it by the fire, Thompson got up and went out.

'Now the difficulty of it was, that I wasn't sure it WAS Thompson, because I had never set eyes on him before; and what I had wanted was to be quite certain of him. However, there was nothing for it now, but to follow, and put a bold face upon it. I found him talking, outside in the yard, with the landlady. It turned out afterwards that he was wanted by a Northampton officer for something else, and that, knowing that officer to be pock-marked (as I am myself), he mistook me for him. As I have observed, I found him talking to the landlady, outside. I put my hand upon his shoulder - this way - and said, "Tally-ho Thompson, it's no use. I know you. I'm an officer from London, and I take you into custody for felony!" "That be d-d!" says Tally-ho Thompson.

'We went back into the house, and the two friends began to cut up rough, and their looks didn't please me at all, I assure you. "Let the man go. What are you going to do with him?" "I'll tell you what I'm going to do with him. I'm going to take him to London to- night, as sure as I'm alive. I'm not alone here, whatever you may think. You mind your own business, and keep yourselves to yourselves. It'll be better for you, for I know you both very well." I'D never seen or heard of 'em in all my life, but my bouncing cowed 'em a bit, and they kept off, while Thompson was making ready to go. I thought to myself, however, that they might be coming after me on the dark road, to rescue Thompson; so I said to the landlady, "What men have you got in the house, Missis?" "We haven't got no men here," she says, sulkily. "You have got an ostler, I suppose?" "Yes, we've got an ostler." "Let me see him." Presently he came, and a shaggy-headed young fellow he was. "Now attend to me, young man," says I;

"I'm a Detective Officer from London. This man's name is Thompson. I have taken him into custody for felony. I am going to take him to the railroad station. I call upon you in the Queen's name to assist me; and mind you, my friend, you'll get yourself into more trouble than you know of, if you don't!' You never saw a person open his eyes so wide. "Now, Thompson, come along!" says I. But when I took out the handcuffs, Thompson cries, "No! None of that! I won't stand THEM! I'll go along with you quiet, but I won't bear none of that!" "Tally-ho Thompson," I said, "I'm willing to behave as a man to you, if you are willing to behave as a man to me. Give me your word that you'll come peaceably along, and I don't want to handcuff you." "I will," says Thompson, "but I'll have a glass of brandy first." "I don't care if I've another," said I. "We'll have two more, Missis," said the friends, "and confound you, Constable, you'll give your man a drop, won't you?" I was agreeable to that, so we had it all round, and then my man and I took Tally-ho Thompson safe to the railroad, and I carried him to London that night. He was afterwards acquitted, on account of a defect in the evidence; and I understand he always praises me up to the skies, and says I'm one of the best of men.'

This story coming to a termination amidst general applause, Inspector Wield, after a little grave smoking, fixes his eye on his host, and thus delivers himself:

'It wasn't a bad plant that of mine, on Fikey, the man accused of forging the Sou'-Western Railway debentures - it was only t'other day - because the reason why? I'll tell you.

'I had information that Fikey and his brother kept a factory over yonder there,' - indicating any region on the Surrey side of the river - 'where he bought second-hand carriages; so after I'd tried in vain to get hold of him by other means, I wrote him a letter in an assumed name, saying that I'd got a horse and shay to dispose of, and would drive down next day that he might view the lot, and make an offer - very reasonable it was, I said - a reg'lar bargain. Straw and me then went off to a friend of mine that's in the livery and job business, and hired a turn-out for the day, a precious smart turn-out it was - quite a slap-up thing! Down we drove, accordingly, with a friend (who's not in the Force himself); and leaving my friend in the shay near a public-house, to take care of the horse, we went to the factory, which was some little way off. In the factory, there was a number of strong fellows at work, and after reckoning 'em up, it was clear to me that it wouldn't do to try it on there. They were too many for us. We must get our man out of doors. "Mr. Fikey at home?" "No, he ain't." "Expected home soon?" "Why, no, not soon." "Ah! Is his brother here?" "I'M his brother." "Oh! well, this is an ill-conwenience, this is. I wrote him a letter yesterday, saying I'd got a little turn-out to dispose of, and I've took the trouble to bring the turn-out down a' purpose, and now he ain't in the way." "No, he ain't in the way. You couldn't make it convenient to call again, could you?" "Why, no, I couldn't. I want to sell; that's the fact; and I can't put it off. Could you find him anywheres?" At first he said No, he couldn't, and then he wasn't sure about it, and then he'd go and try. So at last he went up-stairs, where there was a sort of loft, and presently down comes my man himself in his shirt-sleeves.

'"Well," he says, "this seems to be rayther a pressing matter of yours." "Yes," I says, "it IS rayther a pressing matter, and you'll find it a bargain - dirt cheap." "I ain't in partickler want of a bargain just now," he says, "but where is it?" "Why," I says, "the turn-out's just outside. Come and look at it." He hasn't any suspicions, and away we go. And the first thing that happens is, that the horse runs away with my friend (who knows no more of driving than a child) when he takes a little trot along the road to show his paces. You never saw such a game in your life!

'When the bolt is over, and the turn-out has come to a standstill again, Fikey walks round and round it as grave as a judge - me too. "There, sir!" I says. "There's a neat thing!" "It ain't a bad style of thing," he says. "I believe you," says I. "And there's a horse!" - for I saw him looking at it. "Rising eight!" I says, rubbing his fore-legs. (Bless you, there ain't a man in the world knows less of horses than I do, but I'd heard my friend at the Livery Stables say he was eight year old, so I says, as knowing as possible, "Rising eight.") "Rising eight, is he?" says he. "Rising eight," says I. "Well," he says, "what do you want for it?" "Why, the first and last figure for the whole concern is five-and-twenty pound!" "That's very cheap!" he says, looking at me. "Ain't it?" I says. "I told you it was a bargain! Now, without any higgling and haggling about it, what I want is to sell, and that's my price. Further, I'll make it easy to you, and take half the money down, and you can do a bit of stiff (1) for the balance."

"Well," he says again, "that's very cheap." "I believe you," says I; "get in and try it, and you'll buy it. Come! take a trial!"

'Ecod, he gets in, and we get in, and we drive along the road, to show him to one of the railway clerks that was hid in the public- house window to identify him. But the clerk was bothered, and didn't know whether it was him, or wasn't - because the reason why? I'll tell you, - on account of his having shaved his whiskers. "It's a clever little horse," he says, "and trots well; and the shay runs light." "Not a doubt about it," I says. "And now, Mr. Fikey, I may as well make it all right, without wasting any more of your time. The fact is, I'm Inspector Wield, and you're my prisoner." "You don't mean that?" he says. "I do, indeed." "Then burn my body," says Fikey, "if this ain't TOO bad!"

'Perhaps you never saw a man so knocked over with surprise. "I hope you'll let me have my coat?" he says. "By all means." "Well, then, let's drive to the factory." "Why, not exactly that, I think," said I; "I've been there, once before, to-day. Suppose we send for it." He saw it was no go, so he sent for it, and put it on, and we drove him up to London, comfortable.'

This reminiscence is in the height of its success, when a general proposal is made to the fresh-complexioned, smooth-faced officer, with the strange air of simplicity, to tell the 'Butcher's Story.'

The fresh-complexioned, smooth-faced officer, with the strange air of simplicity, began with a rustic smile, and in a soft, wheedling tone of voice, to relate the Butcher's Story, thus:

'It's just about six years ago, now, since information was given at Scotland Yard of there being extensive robberies of lawns and silks going on, at some wholesale houses in the City. Directions were given for the business being looked into; and Straw, and Fendall, and me, we were all in it.'

'When you received your instructions,' said we, 'you went away, and held a sort of Cabinet Council together!'

The smooth-faced officer coaxingly replied, 'Ye-es. Just so. We turned it over among ourselves a good deal. It appeared, when we went into it, that the goods were sold by the receivers extraordinarily cheap - much cheaper than they could have been if they had been honestly come by. The receivers were in the trade, and kept capital shops - establishments of the first respectability - one of 'em at the West End, one down in Westminster. After a lot of watching and inquiry, and this and that among ourselves, we found that the job was managed, and the purchases of the stolen goods made, at a little public-house near Smithfield, down by Saint Bartholomew's; where the Warehouse Porters, who were the thieves, took 'em for that purpose, don't you see? and made appointments to meet the people that went between themselves and the receivers. This public-house was principally used by journeymen butchers from the country, out of place, and in want of situations; so, what did we do, but - ha, ha, ha! - we agreed that I should be dressed up like a butcher myself, and go and live there!'

Never, surely, was a faculty of observation better brought to bear upon a purpose, than that which picked out this officer for the part. Nothing in all creation could have suited him better. Even while he spoke, he became a greasy, sleepy, shy, good-natured, chuckle-headed, unsuspicious, and confiding young butcher. His very hair seemed to have suet in it, as he made it smooth upon his head, and his fresh complexion to be lubricated by large quantities of animal food.

' - So I - ha, ha, ha!' (always with the confiding snigger of the foolish young butcher) 'so I dressed myself in the regular way, made up a little bundle of clothes, and went to the public-house, and asked if I could have a lodging there? They says, "yes, you can have a lodging here," and I got a bedroom, and settled myself down in the tap. There was a number of people about the place, and coming backwards and forwards to the house; and first one says, and then another says, "Are you from the country, young man?" "Yes," I says, "I am. I'm come out of Northamptonshire, and I'm quite lonely here, for I don't know London at all, and it's such a mighty big town." "It IS a big town," they says. "Oh, it's a VERY big town!" I says. "Really and truly I never was in such a town. It quite confuses of me!" and all that, you know.

'When some of the journeymen Butchers that used the house, found that I wanted a place, they says, "Oh, we'll get you a place!" And they actually took me to a sight of places, in Newgate Market, Newport Market, Clare, Carnaby - I don't know where all. But the wages was - ha, ha, ha! - was not sufficient, and I never could suit myself, don't you see? Some of the queer frequenters of the house were a little suspicious of me at first, and I was obliged to be very cautious indeed how I communicated with Straw or Fendall. Sometimes, when I went out, pretending to stop and look into the shop windows, and just casting my eye round, I used to see some of 'em following me; but, being perhaps better accustomed than they thought for, to that sort of thing, I used to lead 'em on as far as I thought necessary or convenient - sometimes a long way - and then turn sharp round, and meet 'em, and say, "Oh, dear, how glad I am to come upon you so fortunate! This London's such a place, I'm blowed if I ain't lost again!" And then we'd go back all together, to the public-house, and - ha, ha, ha! and smoke our pipes, don't you see?

'They were very attentive to me, I am sure. It was a common thing, while I was living there, for some of 'em to take me out, and show me London. They showed me the Prisons - showed me Newgate - and when they showed me Newgate, I stops at the place where the Porters pitch their loads, and says, "Oh dear, is this where they hang the men? Oh Lor!" "That!" they says, "what a simple cove he is! THAT ain't it!" And then, they pointed out which WAS it, and I says "Lor!" and they says, "Now you'll know it agen, won't you?" And I said I thought I should if I tried hard - and I assure you I kept a sharp look out for the City Police when we were out in this way, for if any of 'em had happened to know me, and had spoke to me, it would have been all up in a minute. However, by good luck such a thing never happened, and all went on quiet: though the difficulties I had in communicating with my brother officers were quite extraordinary.

'The stolen goods that were brought to the public-house by the Warehouse Porters, were always disposed of in a back parlour. For a long time, I never could get into this parlour, or see what was done there. As I sat smoking my pipe, like an innocent young chap, by the tap-room fire, I'd hear some of the parties to the robbery, as they came in and out, say softly to the landlord, "Who's that? What does HE do here?" "Bless your soul," says the landlord, "he's only a" - ha, ha, ha! - "he's only a green young fellow from the country, as is looking for a butcher's sitiwation. Don't mind HIM!" So, in course of time, they were so convinced of my being green, and got to be so accustomed to me, that I was as free of the parlour as any of 'em, and I have seen as much as Seventy Pounds' Worth of fine lawn sold there, in one night, that was stolen from a warehouse in Friday Street. After the sale the buyers always stood treat - hot supper, or dinner, or what not - and they'd say on those occasions, "Come on, Butcher! Put your best leg foremost, young 'un, and walk into it!" Which I used to do - and hear, at table, all manner of particulars that it was very important for us Detectives to know.

'This went on for ten weeks. I lived in the public-house all the time, and never was out of the Butcher's dress - except in bed. At last, when I had followed seven of the thieves, and set 'em to rights - that's an expression of ours, don't you see, by which I mean to say that I traced 'em, and found out where the robberies were done, and all about 'em - Straw, and Fendall, and I, gave one another the office, and at a time agreed upon, a descent was made upon the public-house, and the apprehensions effected. One of the first things the officers did, was to collar me - for the parties to the robbery weren't to suppose yet, that I was anything but a Butcher - on which the landlord cries out, "Don't take HIM," he says, "whatever you do! He's only a poor young chap from the country, and butter wouldn't melt in his mouth!" However, they - ha, ha, ha! - they took me, and pretended to search my bedroom, where nothing was found but an old fiddle belonging to the landlord, that had got there somehow or another. But, it entirely changed the landlord's opinion, for when it was produced, he says, "My fiddle! The Butcher's a purloiner! I give him into custody for the robbery of a musical instrument!"

'The man that had stolen the goods in Friday Street was not taken yet. He had told me, in confidence, that he had his suspicions there was something wrong (on account of the City Police having captured one of the party), and that he was going to make himself scarce. I asked him, "Where do you mean to go, Mr. Shepherdson?" "Why, Butcher," says he, "the Setting Moon, in the Commercial Road, is a snug house, and I shall bang out there for a time. I shall call myself Simpson, which appears to me to be a modest sort of a name. Perhaps you'll give us a look in, Butcher?" "Well," says I, "I think I WILL give you a call" - which I fully intended, don't you see, because, of course, he was to be taken! I went over to the Setting Moon next day, with a brother officer, and asked at the bar for Simpson. They pointed out his room, up-stairs. As we were going up, he looks down over the banister, and calls out, "Halloa, Butcher! is that you?" "Yes, it's me. How do you find yourself?" "Bobbish," he says; "but who's that with you?" "It's only a young man, that's a friend of mine," I says. "Come along, then," says he; "any friend of the Butcher's is as welcome as the Butcher!" So, I made my friend acquainted with him, and we took him into custody.

'You have no idea, sir, what a sight it was, in Court, when they first knew that I wasn't a Butcher, after all! I wasn't produced at the first examination, when there was a remand; but I was at the second. And when I stepped into the box, in full police uniform, and the whole party saw how they had been done, actually a groan of horror and dismay proceeded from 'em in the dock!

'At the Old Bailey, when their trials came on, Mr. Clarkson was engaged for the defence, and he COULDN'T make out how it was, about the Butcher. He thought, all along, it was a real Butcher. When the counsel for the prosecution said, "I will now call before you, gentlemen, the Police-officer," meaning myself, Mr. Clarkson says, "Why Police-officer? Why more Police-officers? I don't want Police. We have had a great deal too much of the Police. I want the Butcher!" However, sir, he had the Butcher and the Police- officer, both in one. Out of seven prisoners committed for trial, five were found guilty, and some of 'em were transported. The respectable firm at the West End got a term of imprisonment; and that's the Butcher's Story!'

The story done, the chuckle-headed Butcher again resolved himself into the smooth-faced Detective. But, he was so extremely tickled by their having taken him about, when he was that Dragon in disguise, to show him London, that he could not help reverting to that point in his narrative; and gently repeating with the Butcher snigger, '"Oh, dear," I says, "is that where they hang the men? Oh, Lor!" "THAT!" says they. "What a simple cove he is!"'

It being now late, and the party very modest in their fear of being too diffuse, there were some tokens of separation; when Sergeant Dornton, the soldierly-looking man, said, looking round him with a smile:

'Before we break up, sir, perhaps you might have some amusement in hearing of the Adventures of a Carpet Bag. They are very short; and, I think, curious.'

We welcomed the Carpet Bag, as cordially as Mr. Shepherdson welcomed the false Butcher at the Setting Moon. Sergeant Dornton proceeded.

'In 1847, I was despatched to Chatham, in search of one Mesheck, a Jew. He had been carrying on, pretty heavily, in the bill-stealing way, getting acceptances from young men of good connexions (in the army chiefly), on pretence of discount, and bolting with the same.

'Mesheck was off, before I got to Chatham. All I could learn about him was, that he had gone, probably to London, and had with him - a Carpet Bag.

'I came back to town, by the last train from Blackwall, and made inquiries concerning a Jew passenger with - a Carpet Bag.

'The office was shut up, it being the last train. There were only two or three porters left. Looking after a Jew with a Carpet Bag, on the Blackwall Railway, which was then the high road to a great Military Depot, was worse than looking after a needle in a hayrick. But it happened that one of these porters had carried, for a certain Jew, to a certain public-house, a certain - Carpet Bag.

'I went to the public-house, but the Jew had only left his luggage there for a few hours, and had called for it in a cab, and taken it away. I put such questions there, and to the porter, as I thought prudent, and got at this description of - the Carpet Bag.

'It was a bag which had, on one side of it, worked in worsted, a green parrot on a stand. A green parrot on a stand was the means by which to identify that - Carpet Bag.

'I traced Mesheck, by means of this green parrot on a stand, to Cheltenham, to Birmingham, to Liverpool, to the Atlantic Ocean. At Liverpool he was too many for me. He had gone to the United States, and I gave up all thoughts of Mesheck, and likewise of his - Carpet Bag.

'Many months afterwards - near a year afterwards - there was a bank in Ireland robbed of seven thousand pounds, by a person of the name of Doctor Dundey, who escaped to America; from which country some of the stolen notes came home. He was supposed to have bought a farm in New Jersey. Under proper management, that estate could be seized and sold, for the benefit of the parties he had defrauded. I was sent off to America for this purpose.

'I landed at Boston. I went on to New York. I found that he had lately changed New York paper-money for New Jersey paper money, and had banked cash in New Brunswick. To take this Doctor Dundey, it was necessary to entrap him into the State of New York, which required a deal of artifice and trouble. At one time, he couldn't be drawn into an appointment. At another time, he appointed to come to meet me, and a New York officer, on a pretext I made; and then his children had the measles. At last he came, per steamboat, and I took him, and lodged him in a New York prison called the Tombs; which I dare say you know, sir?'

Editorial acknowledgment to that effect.

'I went to the Tombs, on the morning after his capture, to attend the examination before the magistrate. I was passing through the magistrate's private room, when, happening to look round me to take notice of the place, as we generally have a habit of doing, I clapped my eyes, in one corner, on a - Carpet Bag.

'What did I see upon that Carpet Bag, if you'll believe me, but a green parrot on a stand, as large as life!

'"That Carpet Bag, with the representation of a green parrot on a stand," said I, "belongs to an English Jew, named Aaron Mesheck, and to no other man, alive or dead!"

'I give you my word the New York Police Officers were doubled up with surprise.

'"How did you ever come to know that?" said they.

'"I think I ought to know that green parrot by this time," said I; "for I have had as pretty a dance after that bird, at home, as ever I had, in all my life!"'

'And was it Mesheck's?' we submissively inquired.

'Was it, sir? Of course it was! He was in custody for another offence, in that very identical Tombs, at that very identical time. And, more than that! Some memoranda, relating to the fraud for which I had vainly endeavoured to take him, were found to be, at that moment, lying in that very same individual - Carpet Bag!'

Such are the curious coincidences and such is the peculiar ability, always sharpening and being improved by practice, and always adapting itself to every variety of circumstances, and opposing itself to every new device that perverted ingenuity can invent, for which this important social branch of the public service is remarkable! For ever on the watch, with their wits stretched to the utmost, these officers have, from day to day and year to year, to set themselves against every novelty of trickery and dexterity that the combined imaginations of all the lawless rascals in England can devise, and to keep pace with every such invention that comes out. In the Courts of Justice, the materials of thousands of such stories as we have narrated - often elevated into the marvellous and romantic, by the circumstances of the case - are dryly compressed into the set phrase, 'in consequence of information I received, I did so and so.' Suspicion was to be directed, by careful inference and deduction, upon the right person; the right person was to be taken, wherever he had gone, or whatever he was doing to avoid detection: he is taken; there he is at the bar; that is enough. From information I, the officer, received, I did it; and, according to the custom in these cases, I say no more.

These games of chess, played with live pieces, are played before small audiences, and are chronicled nowhere. The interest of the game supports the player. Its results are enough for justice. To compare great things with small, suppose LEVERRIER or ADAMS informing the public that from information he had received he had discovered a new planet; or COLUMBUS informing the public of his day that from information he had received he had discovered a new continent; so the Detectives inform it that they have discovered a new fraud or an old offender, and the process is unknown.

Thus, at midnight, closed the proceedings of our curious and interesting party. But one other circumstance finally wound up the evening, after our Detective guests had left us. One of the sharpest among them, and the officer best acquainted with the Swell Mob, had his pocket picked, going home!

Footnotes: (1) Give a bill

On Duty with Inspector Field

How goes the night? Saint Giles's clock is striking nine. The weather is dull and wet, and the long lines of street lamps are blurred, as if we saw them through tears. A damp wind blows and rakes the pieman's fire out, when he opens the door of his little furnace, carrying away an eddy of sparks.

Saint Giles's clock strikes nine. We are punctual. Where is Inspector Field? Assistant Commissioner of Police is already here, enwrapped in oil-skin cloak, and standing in the shadow of Saint Giles's steeple. Detective Sergeant, weary of speaking French all day to foreigners unpacking at the Great Exhibition, is already here. Where is Inspector Field?

Inspector Field is, to-night, the guardian genius of the British Museum. He is bringing his shrewd eye to bear on every corner of its solitary galleries, before he reports 'all right.' Suspicious of the Elgin marbles, and not to be done by cat-faced Egyptian giants with their hands upon their knees, Inspector Field, sagacious, vigilant, lamp in hand, throwing monstrous shadows on the walls and ceilings, passes through the spacious rooms. If a mummy trembled in an atom of its dusty covering, Inspector Field would say, 'Come out of that, Tom Green. I know you!' If the smallest 'Gonoph' about town were crouching at the bottom of a classic bath, Inspector Field would nose him with a finer scent than the ogre's, when adventurous Jack lay trembling in his kitchen copper. But all is quiet, and Inspector Field goes warily on, making little outward show of attending to anything in particular, just recognising the Ichthyosaurus as a familiar acquaintance, and wondering, perhaps, how the detectives did it in the days before the Flood.

Will Inspector Field be long about this work? He may be half-an- hour longer. He sends his compliments by Police Constable, and proposes that we meet at St. Giles's Station House, across the road. Good. It were as well to stand by the fire, there, as in the shadow of Saint Giles's steeple.

Anything doing here to-night? Not much. We are very quiet. A lost boy, extremely calm and small, sitting by the fire, whom we now confide to a constable to take home, for the child says that if you show him Newgate Street, he can show you where he lives - a raving drunken woman in the cells, who has screeched her voice away, and has hardly power enough left to declare, even with the passionate help of her feet and arms, that she is the daughter of a British officer, and, strike her blind and dead, but she'll write a letter to the Queen! but who is soothed with a drink of water - in another cell, a quiet woman with a child at her breast, for begging - in another, her husband in a smock-frock, with a basket of watercresses - in another, a pickpocket - in another, a meek tremulous old pauper man who has been out for a holiday 'and has took but a little drop, but it has overcome him after so many months in the house' - and that's all as yet. Presently, a sensation at the Station House door. Mr. Field, gentlemen!

Inspector Field comes in, wiping his forehead, for he is of a burly figure, and has come fast from the ores and metals of the deep mines of the earth, and from the Parrot Gods of the South Sea Islands, and from the birds and beetles of the tropics, and from the Arts of Greece and Rome, and from the Sculptures of Nineveh, and from the traces of an elder world, when these were not. Is Rogers ready? Rogers is ready, strapped and great-coated, with a flaming eye in the middle of his waist, like a deformed Cyclops. Lead on, Rogers, to Rats' Castle!

How many people may there be in London, who, if we had brought them deviously and blindfold, to this street, fifty paces from the Station House, and within call of Saint Giles's church, would know it for a not remote part of the city in which their lives are passed? How many, who amidst this compound of sickening smells, these heaps of filth, these tumbling houses, with all their vile contents, animate, and inanimate, slimily overflowing into the black road, would believe that they breathe THIS air? How much Red Tape may there be, that could look round on the faces which now hem us in - for our appearance here has caused a rush from all points to a common centre - the lowering foreheads, the sallow cheeks, the brutal eyes, the matted hair, the infected, vermin-haunted heaps of rags - and say, 'I have thought of this. I have not dismissed the thing. I have neither blustered it away, nor frozen it away, nor tied it up and put it away, nor smoothly said pooh, pooh! to it when it has been shown to me?'

This is not what Rogers wants to know, however. What Rogers wants to know, is, whether you WILL clear the way here, some of you, or whether you won't; because if you don't do it right on end, he'll lock you up! 'What! YOU are there, are you, Bob Miles? You haven't had enough of it yet, haven't you? You want three months more, do you? Come away from that gentleman! What are you creeping round there for?'

'What am I a doing, thinn, Mr. Rogers?' says Bob Miles, appearing, villainous, at the end of a lane of light, made by the lantern.

'I'll let you know pretty quick, if you don't hook it. WILL you hook it?'

A sycophantic murmur rises from the crowd. 'Hook it, Bob, when Mr. Rogers and Mr. Field tells you! Why don't you hook it, when you are told to?'

The most importunate of the voices strikes familiarly on Mr. Rogers's ear. He suddenly turns his lantern on the owner.

'What! YOU are there, are you, Mister Click? You hook it too - come!'

'What for?' says Mr. Click, discomfited.

'You hook it, will you!' says Mr. Rogers with stern emphasis.

Both Click and Miles DO 'hook it,' without another word, or, in plainer English, sneak away.

'Close up there, my men!' says Inspector Field to two constables on duty who have followed. 'Keep together, gentlemen; we are going down here. Heads!'

Saint Giles's church strikes half-past ten. We stoop low, and creep down a precipitous flight of steps into a dark close cellar. There is a fire. There is a long deal table. There are benches. The cellar is full of company, chiefly very young men in various conditions of dirt and raggedness. Some are eating supper. There are no girls or women present. Welcome to Rats' Castle, gentlemen, and to this company of noted thieves!

'Well, my lads! How are you, my lads? What have you been doing to-day? Here's some company come to see you, my lads! - THERE'S a plate of beefsteak, sir, for the supper of a fine young man! And there's a mouth for a steak, sir! Why, I should be too proud of such a mouth as that, if I had it myself! Stand up and show it, sir! Take off your cap. There's a fine young man for a nice little party, sir! An't he?'

Inspector Field is the bustling speaker. Inspector Field's eye is the roving eye that searches every corner of the cellar as he talks. Inspector Field's hand is the well-known hand that has collared half the people here, and motioned their brothers, sisters, fathers, mothers, male and female friends, inexorably to New South Wales. Yet Inspector Field stands in this den, the Sultan of the place. Every thief here cowers before him, like a schoolboy before his schoolmaster. All watch him, all answer when addressed, all laugh at his jokes, all seek to propitiate him. This cellar company alone - to say nothing of the crowd surrounding the entrance from the street above, and making the steps shine with eyes - is strong enough to murder us all, and willing enough to do it; but, let Inspector Field have a mind to pick out one thief here, and take him; let him produce that ghostly truncheon from his pocket, and say, with his business-air, 'My lad, I want you!' and all Rats' Castle shall be stricken with paralysis, and not a finger move against him, as he fits the handcuffs on!

Where's the Earl of Warwick? - Here he is, Mr. Field! Here's the Earl of Warwick, Mr. Field! - O there you are, my Lord. Come for'ard. There's a chest, sir, not to have a clean shirt on. An't it? Take your hat off, my Lord. Why, I should be ashamed if I was you - and an Earl, too - to show myself to a gentleman with my hat on! - The Earl of Warwick laughs and uncovers. All the company laugh. One pickpocket, especially, laughs with great enthusiasm. O what a jolly game it is, when Mr. Field comes down - and don't want nobody!

So, YOU are here, too, are you, you tall, grey, soldierly-looking, grave man, standing by the fire? - Yes, sir. Good evening, Mr. Field! - Let us see. You lived servant to a nobleman once? - Yes, Mr. Field. - And what is it you do now; I forget? - Well, Mr. Field, I job about as well as I can. I left my employment on account of delicate health. The family is still kind to me. Mr. Wix of Piccadilly is also very kind to me when I am hard up. Likewise Mr. Nix of Oxford Street. I get a trifle from them occasionally, and rub on as well as I can, Mr. Field. Mr. Field's eye rolls enjoyingly, for this man is a notorious begging-letter writer. - Good night, my lads! - Good night, Mr. Field, and thank'ee, sir!

Clear the street here, half a thousand of you! Cut it, Mrs. Stalker - none of that - we don't want you! Rogers of the flaming eye, lead on to the tramps' lodging-house!

A dream of baleful faces attends to the door. Now, stand back all of you! In the rear Detective Sergeant plants himself, composedly whistling, with his strong right arm across the narrow passage. Mrs. Stalker, I am something'd that need not be written here, if you won't get yourself into trouble, in about half a minute, if I see that face of yours again!

Saint Giles's church clock, striking eleven, hums through our hand from the dilapidated door of a dark outhouse as we open it, and are stricken back by the pestilent breath that issues from within. Rogers to the front with the light, and let us look!

Ten, twenty, thirty - who can count them! Men, women, children, for the most part naked, heaped upon the floor like maggots in a cheese! Ho! In that dark corner yonder! Does anybody lie there? Me sir, Irish me, a widder, with six children. And yonder? Me sir, Irish me, with me wife and eight poor babes. And to the left there? Me sir, Irish me, along with two more Irish boys as is me friends. And to the right there? Me sir and the Murphy fam'ly, numbering five blessed souls. And what's this, coiling, now, about my foot? Another Irish me, pitifully in want of shaving, whom I have awakened from sleep - and across my other foot lies his wife - and by the shoes of Inspector Field lie their three eldest - and their three youngest are at present squeezed between the open door and the wall. And why is there no one on that little mat before the sullen fire? Because O'Donovan, with his wife and daughter, is not come in from selling Lucifers! Nor on the bit of sacking in the nearest corner? Bad luck! Because that Irish family is late to-night, a-cadging in the streets!

They are all awake now, the children excepted, and most of them sit up, to stare. Wheresoever Mr. Rogers turns the flaming eye, there is a spectral figure rising, unshrouded, from a grave of rags. Who is the landlord here? - I am, Mr. Field! says a bundle of ribs and parchment against the wall, scratching itself. - Will you spend this money fairly, in the morning, to buy coffee for 'em all? - Yes, sir, I will! - O he'll do it, sir, he'll do it fair. He's honest! cry the spectres. And with thanks and Good Night sink into their graves again.

Thus, we make our New Oxford Streets, and our other new streets, never heeding, never asking, where the wretches whom we clear out, crowd. With such scenes at our doors, with all the plagues of Egypt tied up with bits of cobweb in kennels so near our homes, we timorously make our Nuisance Bills and Boards of Health, nonentities, and think to keep away the Wolves of Crime and Filth, by our electioneering ducking to little vestrymen and our gentlemanly handling of Red Tape!

Intelligence of the coffee-money has got abroad. The yard is full, and Rogers of the flaming eye is beleaguered with entreaties to show other Lodging Houses. Mine next! Mine! Mine! Rogers, military, obdurate, stiff-necked, immovable, replies not, but leads away; all falling back before him. Inspector Field follows. Detective Sergeant, with his barrier of arm across the little passage, deliberately waits to close the procession. He sees behind him, without any effort, and exceedingly disturbs one individual far in the rear by coolly calling out, 'It won't do, Mr. Michael! Don't try it!'

After council holden in the street, we enter other lodging-houses, public-houses, many lairs and holes; all noisome and offensive; none so filthy and so crowded as where Irish are. In one, The Ethiopian party are expected home presently - were in Oxford Street when last heard of - shall be fetched, for our delight, within ten minutes. In another, one of the two or three Professors who drew Napoleon Buonaparte and a couple of mackerel, on the pavement and then let the work of art out to a speculator, is refreshing after his labours. In another, the vested interest of the profitable nuisance has been in one family for a hundred years, and the landlord drives in comfortably from the country to his snug little stew in town. In all, Inspector Field is received with warmth. Coiners and smashers droop before him; pickpockets defer to him; the gentle sex (not very gentle here) smile upon him. Half-drunken hags check themselves in the midst of pots of beer, or pints of gin, to drink to Mr. Field, and pressingly to ask the honour of his finishing the draught. One beldame in rusty black has such admiration for him, that she runs a whole street's length to shake him by the hand; tumbling into a heap of mud by the way, and still pressing her attentions when her very form has ceased to be distinguishable through it. Before the power of the law, the power of superior sense - for common thieves are fools beside these men - and the power of a perfect mastery of their character, the garrison of Rats' Castle and the adjacent Fortresses make but a skulking show indeed when reviewed by Inspector Field.

Saint Giles's clock says it will be midnight in half-an-hour, and Inspector Field says we must hurry to the Old Mint in the Borough. The cab-driver is low-spirited, and has a solemn sense of his responsibility. Now, what's your fare, my lad? - O YOU know, Inspector Field, what's the good of asking ME!

Say, Parker, strapped and great-coated, and waiting in dim Borough doorway by appointment, to replace the trusty Rogers whom we left deep in Saint Giles's, are you ready? Ready, Inspector Field, and at a motion of my wrist behold my flaming eye.

This narrow street, sir, is the chief part of the Old Mint, full of low lodging-houses, as you see by the transparent canvas-lamps and blinds, announcing beds for travellers! But it is greatly changed, friend Field, from my former knowledge of it; it is infinitely quieter and more subdued than when I was here last, some seven years ago? O yes! Inspector Haynes, a first-rate man, is on this station now and plays the Devil with them!

Well, my lads! How are you to-night, my lads? Playing cards here, eh? Who wins? - Why, Mr. Field, I, the sulky gentleman with the damp flat side-curls, rubbing my bleared eye with the end of my neckerchief which is like a dirty eel-skin, am losing just at present, but I suppose I must take my pipe out of my mouth, and be submissive to YOU - I hope I see you well, Mr. Field? - Aye, all right, my lad. Deputy, who have you got up-stairs? Be pleased to show the rooms!

Why Deputy, Inspector Field can't say. He only knows that the man who takes care of the beds and lodgers is always called so. Steady, O Deputy, with the flaring candle in the blacking-bottle, for this is a slushy back-yard, and the wooden staircase outside the house creaks and has holes in it.

Again, in these confined intolerable rooms, burrowed out like the holes of rats or the nests of insect-vermin, but fuller of intolerable smells, are crowds of sleepers, each on his foul truckle-bed coiled up beneath a rug. Holloa here! Come! Let us see you! Show your face! Pilot Parker goes from bed to bed and turns their slumbering heads towards us, as a salesman might turn sheep. Some wake up with an execration and a threat. - What! who spoke? O! If it's the accursed glaring eye that fixes me, go where I will, I am helpless. Here! I sit up to be looked at. Is it me you want? Not you, lie down again! and I lie down, with a woful growl.

Whenever the turning lane of light becomes stationary for a moment, some sleeper appears at the end of it, submits himself to be scrutinised, and fades away into the darkness.

There should be strange dreams here, Deputy. They sleep sound enough, says Deputy, taking the candle out of the blacking-bottle, snuffing it with his fingers, throwing the snuff into the bottle, and corking it up with the candle; that's all I know. What is the inscription, Deputy, on all the discoloured sheets? A precaution against loss of linen. Deputy turns down the rug of an unoccupied bed and discloses it. STOP THIEF!

To lie at night, wrapped in the legend of my slinking life; to take the cry that pursues me, waking, to my breast in sleep; to have it staring at me, and clamouring for me, as soon as consciousness returns; to have it for my first-foot on New-Year's day, my Valentine, my Birthday salute, my Christmas greeting, my parting with the old year. STOP THIEF!

And to know that I MUST be stopped, come what will. To know that I am no match for this individual energy and keenness, or this organised and steady system! Come across the street, here, and, entering by a little shop and yard, examine these intricate passages and doors, contrived for escape, flapping and counter- flapping, like the lids of the conjurer's boxes. But what avail they? Who gets in by a nod, and shows their secret working to us? Inspector Field.

Don't forget the old Farm House, Parker! Parker is not the man to forget it. We are going there, now. It is the old Manor-House of these parts, and stood in the country once. Then, perhaps, there was something, which was not the beastly street, to see from the shattered low fronts of the overhanging wooden houses we are passing under - shut up now, pasted over with bills about the literature and drama of the Mint, and mouldering away. This long paved yard was a paddock or a garden once, or a court in front of the Farm House. Perchance, with a dovecot in the centre, and fowls peeking about - with fair elm trees, then, where discoloured chimney-stacks and gables are now - noisy, then, with rooks which have yielded to a different sort of rookery. It's likelier than not, Inspector Field thinks, as we turn into the common kitchen, which is in the yard, and many paces from the house.

Well, my lads and lasses, how are you all? Where's Blackey, who has stood near London Bridge these five-and-twenty years, with a painted skin to represent disease? - Here he is, Mr. Field! - How are you, Blackey? - Jolly, sa! Not playing the fiddle to-night, Blackey? - Not a night, sa! A sharp, smiling youth, the wit of the kitchen, interposes. He an't musical to-night, sir. I've been giving him a moral lecture; I've been a talking to him about his latter end, you see. A good many of these are my pupils, sir. This here young man (smoothing down the hair of one near him, reading a Sunday paper) is a pupil of mine. I'm a teaching of him to read, sir. He's a promising cove, sir. He's a smith, he is, and gets his living by the sweat of the brow, sir. So do I, myself, sir. This young woman is my sister, Mr. Field. SHE'S getting on very well too. I've a deal of trouble with 'em, sir, but I'm richly rewarded, now I see 'em all a doing so well, and growing up so creditable. That's a great comfort, that is, an't it, sir? - In the midst of the kitchen (the whole kitchen is in ecstasies with this impromptu 'chaff') sits a young, modest, gentle-looking creature, with a beautiful child in her lap. She seems to belong to the company, but is so strangely unlike it. She has such a pretty, quiet face and voice, and is so proud to hear the child admired - thinks you would hardly believe that he is only nine months old! Is she as bad as the rest, I wonder? Inspectorial experience does not engender a belief contrariwise, but prompts the answer, Not a ha'porth of difference!

There is a piano going in the old Farm House as we approach. It stops. Landlady appears. Has no objections, Mr. Field, to gentlemen being brought, but wishes it were at earlier hours, the lodgers complaining of ill-convenience. Inspector Field is polite and soothing - knows his woman and the sex. Deputy (a girl in this case) shows the way up a heavy, broad old staircase, kept very clean, into clean rooms where many sleepers are, and where painted panels of an older time look strangely on the truckle beds. The sight of whitewash and the smell of soap - two things we seem by this time to have parted from in infancy - make the old Farm House a phenomenon, and connect themselves with the so curiously misplaced picture of the pretty mother and child long after we have left it, - long after we have left, besides, the neighbouring nook with something of a rustic flavour in it yet, where once, beneath a low wooden colonnade still standing as of yore, the eminent Jack Sheppard condescended to regale himself, and where, now, two old bachelor brothers in broad hats (who are whispered in the Mint to have made a compact long ago that if either should ever marry, he must forfeit his share of the joint property) still keep a sequestered tavern, and sit o' nights smoking pipes in the bar, among ancient bottles and glasses, as our eyes behold them.

How goes the night now? Saint George of Southwark answers with twelve blows upon his bell. Parker, good night, for Williams is already waiting over in the region of Ratcliffe Highway, to show the houses where the sailors dance.

I should like to know where Inspector Field was born. In Ratcliffe Highway, I would have answered with confidence, but for his being equally at home wherever we go. HE does not trouble his head as I do, about the river at night. HE does not care for its creeping, black and silent, on our right there, rushing through sluice-gates, lapping at piles and posts and iron rings, hiding strange things in its mud, running away with suicides and accidentally drowned bodies faster than midnight funeral should, and acquiring such various experience between its cradle and its grave. It has no mystery for HIM. Is there not the Thames Police!

Accordingly, Williams leads the way. We are a little late, for some of the houses are already closing. No matter. You show us plenty. All the landlords know Inspector Field. All pass him, freely and good-humouredly, wheresoever he wants to go. So thoroughly are all these houses open to him and our local guide, that, granting that sailors must be entertained in their own way - as I suppose they must, and have a right to be - I hardly know how such places could be better regulated. Not that I call the company very select, or the dancing very graceful - even so graceful as that of the German Sugar Bakers, whose assembly, by the Minories, we stopped to visit - but there is watchful maintenance of order in every house, and swift expulsion where need is. Even in the midst of drunkenness, both of the lethargic kind and the lively, there is sharp landlord supervision, and pockets are in less peril than out of doors. These houses show, singularly, how much of the picturesque and romantic there truly is in the sailor, requiring to be especially addressed. All the songs (sung in a hailstorm of halfpence, which are pitched at the singer without the least tenderness for the time or tune - mostly from great rolls of copper carried for the purpose - and which he occasionally dodges like shot as they fly near his head) are of the sentimental sea sort. All the rooms are decorated with nautical subjects. Wrecks, engagements, ships on fire, ships passing lighthouses on iron-bound coasts, ships blowing up, ships going down, ships running ashore, men lying out upon the main-yard in a gale of wind, sailors and ships in every variety of peril, constitute the illustrations of fact. Nothing can be done in the fanciful way, without a thumping boy upon a scaly dolphin.

How goes the night now? Past one. Black and Green are waiting in Whitechapel to unveil the mysteries of Wentworth Street. Williams, the best of friends must part. Adieu!

Are not Black and Green ready at the appointed place? O yes! They glide out of shadow as we stop. Imperturbable Black opens the cab- door; Imperturbable Green takes a mental note of the driver. Both Green and Black then open each his flaming eye, and marshal us the way that we are going.

The lodging-house we want is hidden in a maze of streets and courts. It is fast shut. We knock at the door, and stand hushed looking up for a light at one or other of the begrimed old lattice windows in its ugly front, when another constable comes up - supposes that we want 'to see the school.' Detective Sergeant meanwhile has got over a rail, opened a gate, dropped down an area, overcome some other little obstacles, and tapped at a window. Now returns. The landlord will send a deputy immediately.

Deputy is heard to stumble out of bed. Deputy lights a candle, draws back a bolt or two, and appears at the door. Deputy is a shivering shirt and trousers by no means clean, a yawning face, a shock head much confused externally and internally. We want to look for some one. You may go up with the light, and take 'em all, if you like, says Deputy, resigning it, and sitting down upon a bench in the kitchen with his ten fingers sleepily twisting in his hair.

Halloa here! Now then! Show yourselves. That'll do. It's not you. Don't disturb yourself any more! So on, through a labyrinth of airless rooms, each man responding, like a wild beast, to the keeper who has tamed him, and who goes into his cage. What, you haven't found him, then? says Deputy, when we came down. A woman mysteriously sitting up all night in the dark by the smouldering ashes of the kitchen fire, says it's only tramps and cadgers here; it's gonophs over the way. A man mysteriously walking about the kitchen all night in the dark, bids her hold her tongue. We come out. Deputy fastens the door and goes to bed again.

Black and Green, you know Bark, lodging-house keeper and receiver of stolen goods? - O yes, Inspector Field. - Go to Bark's next.

Bark sleeps in an inner wooden hutch, near his street door. As we parley on the step with Bark's Deputy, Bark growls in his bed. We enter, and Bark flies out of bed. Bark is a red villain and a wrathful, with a sanguine throat that looks very much as if it were expressly made for hanging, as he stretches it out, in pale defiance, over the half-door of his hutch. Bark's parts of speech are of an awful sort - principally adjectives. I won't, says Bark, have no adjective police and adjective strangers in my adjective premises! I won't, by adjective and substantive! Give me my trousers, and I'll send the whole adjective police to adjective and substantive! Give me, says Bark, my adjective trousers! I'll put an adjective knife in the whole bileing of 'em. I'll punch their adjective heads. I'll rip up their adjective substantives. Give me my adjective trousers! says Bark, and I'll spile the bileing of 'em!

Now, Bark, what's the use of this? Here's Black and Green, Detective Sergeant, and Inspector Field. You know we will come in. - I know you won't! says Bark. Somebody give me my adjective trousers! Bark's trousers seem difficult to find. He calls for them as Hercules might for his club. Give me my adjective trousers! says Bark, and I'll spile the bileing of 'em!

Inspector Field holds that it's all one whether Bark likes the visit or don't like it. He, Inspector Field, is an Inspector of the Detective Police, Detective Sergeant IS Detective Sergeant, Black and Green are constables in uniform. Don't you be a fool, Bark, or you know it will be the worse for you. - I don't care, says Bark. Give me my adjective trousers!

At two o'clock in the morning, we descend into Bark's low kitchen, leaving Bark to foam at the mouth above, and Imperturbable Black and Green to look at him. Bark's kitchen is crammed full of thieves, holding a CONVERSAZIONE there by lamp-light. It is by far the most dangerous assembly we have seen yet. Stimulated by the ravings of Bark, above, their looks are sullen, but not a man speaks. We ascend again. Bark has got his trousers, and is in a state of madness in the passage with his back against a door that shuts off the upper staircase. We observe, in other respects, a ferocious individuality in Bark. Instead of 'STOP THIEF!' on his linen, he prints 'STOLEN FROM Bark's!'

Now, Bark, we are going up-stairs! - No, you ain't! - YOU refuse admission to the Police, do you, Bark? - Yes, I do! I refuse it to all the adjective police, and to all the adjective substantives. If the adjective coves in the kitchen was men, they'd come up now, and do for you! Shut me that there door! says Bark, and suddenly we are enclosed in the passage. They'd come up and do for you! cries Bark, and waits. Not a sound in the kitchen! They'd come up and do for you! cries Bark again, and waits. Not a sound in the kitchen! We are shut up, half-a-dozen of us, in Bark's house in the innermost recesses of the worst part of London, in the dead of the night - the house is crammed with notorious robbers and ruffians - and not a man stirs. No, Bark. They know the weight of the law, and they know Inspector Field and Co. too well.

We leave bully Bark to subside at leisure out of his passion and his trousers, and, I dare say, to be inconveniently reminded of this little brush before long. Black and Green do ordinary duty here, and look serious.

As to White, who waits on Holborn Hill to show the courts that are eaten out of Rotten Gray's Inn, Lane, where other lodging-houses are, and where (in one blind alley) the Thieves' Kitchen and Seminary for the teaching of the art to children is, the night has so worn away, being now almost at odds with morning, which is which,

that they are quiet, and no light shines through the chinks in the shutters. As undistinctive Death will come here, one day, sleep comes now. The wicked cease from troubling sometimes, even in this life.

The Trial For Murder

I have always noticed a prevalent want of courage, even among persons of superior intelligence and culture, as to imparting their own psychological experiences when those have been of a strange sort. Almost all men are afraid that what they could relate in such wise would find no parallel or response in a listener's internal life, and might be suspected or laughed at. A truthful traveller, who should have seen some extraordinary creature in the likeness of a sea-serpent, would have no fear of mentioning it; but the same traveller, having had some singular presentiment, impulse, vagary of thought, vision (so-called), dream, or other remarkable mental impression, would hesitate considerably before he would own to it. To this reticence I attribute much of the obscurity in which such subjects are involved. We do not habitually communicate our experiences of these subjective things as we do our experiences of objective creation. The consequence is, that the general stock of experience in this regard appears exceptional, and really is so, in respect of being miserably imperfect.

In what I am going to relate, I have no intention of setting up, opposing, or supporting, any theory whatever. I know the history of the Bookseller of Berlin, I have studied the case of the wife of a late Astronomer Royal as related by Sir David Brewster, and I have followed the minutest details of a much more remarkable case of Spectral Illusion occurring within my private circle of friends. It may be necessary to state as to this last, that the sufferer (a lady) was in no degree, however distant, related to me. A mistaken assumption on that head might suggest an explanation of a part of my own case, but only a part, which would be wholly without foundation. It cannot be referred to my inheritance of any developed peculiarity, nor had I ever before any at all similar experience, nor have I ever had any at all similar experience since.

It does not signify how many years ago, or how few, a certain murder was committed in England, which attracted great attention. We hear more than enough of murderers as they rise in succession to their atrocious eminence, and I would bury the memory of this particular brute, if I could, as his body was buried, in Newgate Jail. I purposely abstain from giving any direct clue to the criminal's individuality.

When the murder was first discovered, no suspicion fell, or I ought rather to say, for I cannot be too precise in my facts, it was nowhere publicly hinted that any suspicion fell on the man who was afterwards brought to trial. As no reference was at that time made to him in the newspapers, it is obviously impossible that any description of him can at that time have been given in the newspapers. It is essential that this fact be remembered.

Unfolding at breakfast my morning paper, containing the account of that first discovery, I found it to be deeply interesting, and I read it with close attention. I read it twice, if not three times. The discovery had been made in a bedroom, and, when I laid down the paper, I was aware of a flash, rush, flow, I do not know what to call it, no word I can find is satisfactorily descriptive, in which I seemed to see that bedroom passing through my room, like a picture impossibly painted on a running river. Though almost instantaneous in its passing, it was perfectly clear; so clear that I distinctly, and with a sense of relief, observed the absence of the dead body from the bed.

It was in no romantic place that I had this curious sensation, but in chambers in Piccadilly, very near to the corner of St. James's Street. It was entirely new to me. I was in my easy-chair at the moment, and the sensation was accompanied with a peculiar shiver which started the chair from its position. (But it is to be noted that the chair ran easily on castors.) I went to one of the windows (there are two in the room, and the room is on the second floor) to refresh my eyes with the moving objects down in Piccadilly. It was a bright autumn morning, and the street was sparkling and cheerful. The wind was high. As I looked out, it brought down from the Park a quantity of fallen leaves, which a gust took, and whirled into a spiral pillar. As the pillar fell and the leaves dispersed, I saw two men on the opposite side of the way, going from West to East. They were one behind the other. The foremost man often looked back over his shoulder. The second man followed him, at a distance of some thirty paces, with his right hand menacingly raised. First, the singularity and steadiness of this threatening gesture in so public a thoroughfare attracted my attention; and next, the more remarkable circumstance that nobody heeded it. Both men threaded their way among the other passengers with a smoothness hardly consistent even with the action of walking on a pavement; and no single creature, that I could see, gave them place, touched them, or looked after them. In passing before my windows, they both stared up at me. I saw their two faces very distinctly, and I knew that I could recognise them anywhere. Not that I had consciously noticed anything very remarkable in either face, except that the man who went first had an unusually lowering appearance, and that the face of the man who followed him was of the colour of impure wax.

I am a bachelor, and my valet and his wife constitute my whole establishment. My occupation is in a certain Branch Bank, and I wish that my duties as head of a Department were as light as they are popularly supposed to be. They kept me in town that autumn, when I stood in need of change. I was not ill, but I was not well. My reader is to make the most that can be reasonably made of my feeling jaded, having a depressing sense upon me of a monotonous life, and being "slightly dyspeptic." I am assured by my renowned doctor that my real state of health at that time justifies no stronger description, and I quote his own from his written answer to my request for it.

As the circumstances of the murder, gradually unravelling, took stronger and stronger possession of the public mind, I kept them away from mine by knowing as little about them as was possible in the midst of the universal excitement. But I knew that a verdict of Wilful Murder had been found against the suspected murderer, and that he had been committed to Newgate for trial. I also knew that his trial had been postponed over one Sessions of the Central Criminal Court, on the ground of general prejudice and want of time for the preparation of the defence. I may further have known, but I believe I did not, when, or about when, the Sessions to which his trial stood postponed would come on.

My sitting-room, bedroom, and dressing-room, are all on one floor. With the last there is no communication but through the bedroom. True, there is a door in it, once communicating with the staircase; but a part of the fitting of my bath has been and had then been for some years fixed across it. At the same period, and as a part of the same arrangement, the door had been nailed up and canvased over.

I was standing in my bedroom late one night, giving some directions to my servant before he went to bed. My face was towards the only available door of communication with the dressing-room, and it was closed. My servant's back was towards that door. While I was speaking to him, I saw it open, and a man look in, who very earnestly and mysteriously beckoned to me. That man was the man who had gone second of the two along Piccadilly, and whose face was of the colour of impure wax.

The figure, having beckoned, drew back, and closed the door. With no longer pause than was made by my crossing the bedroom, I opened the dressing-room door, and looked in. I had a lighted candle already in my hand. I felt no inward expectation of seeing the figure in the dressing-room, and I did not see it there.

Conscious that my servant stood amazed, I turned round to him, and said: "Derrick, could you believe that in my cool senses I fancied I saw a" As I there laid my hand upon his breast, with a sudden start he trembled violently, and said, "O Lord, yes, sir! A dead man beckoning!"

Now I do not believe that this John Derrick, my trusty and attached servant for more than twenty years, had any impression whatever of having seen any such figure, until I touched him. The change in him was so startling, when I touched him, that I fully believe he derived his impression in some occult manner from me at that instant.

I bade John Derrick bring some brandy, and I gave him a dram, and was glad to take one myself. Of what had preceded that night's phenomenon, I told him not a single word. Reflecting on it, I was absolutely certain that I had never seen that face before, except on the one occasion in Piccadilly. Comparing its expression when beckoning at the door with its expression when it had stared up at me as I stood at my window, I came to the conclusion that on the first occasion it had sought to fasten itself upon my memory, and that on the second occasion it had made sure of being immediately remembered.

I was not very comfortable that night, though I felt a certainty, difficult to explain, that the figure would not return. At daylight I fell into a heavy sleep, from which I was awakened by John Derrick's coming to my bedside with a paper in his hand.

This paper, it appeared, had been the subject of an altercation at the door between its bearer and my servant. It was a summons to me to serve upon a Jury at the forthcoming Sessions of the Central Criminal Court at the Old Bailey. I had never before been summoned on such a Jury, as John Derrick well knew. He believed, I am not certain at this hour whether with reason or otherwise, that that class of

Jurors were customarily chosen on a lower qualification than mine, and he had at first refused to accept the summons. The man who served it had taken the matter very coolly. He had said that my attendance or non-attendance was nothing to him; there the summons was; and I should deal with it at my own peril, and not at his.

For a day or two I was undecided whether to respond to this call, or take no notice of it. I was not conscious of the slightest mysterious bias, influence, or attraction, one way or other. Of that I am as strictly sure as of every other statement that I make here. Ultimately I decided, as a break in the monotony of my life, that I would go.

The appointed morning was a raw morning in the month of November. There was a dense brown fog in Piccadilly, and it became positively black and in the last degree oppressive East of Temple Bar. I found the passages and staircases of the Court-House flaringly lighted with gas, and the Court itself similarly illuminated. I THINK that, until I was conducted by officers into the Old Court and saw its crowded state, I did not know that the Murderer was to be tried that day. I THINK that, until I was so helped into the Old Court with considerable difficulty, I did not know into which of the two Courts sitting my summons would take me. But this must not be received as a positive assertion, for I am not completely satisfied in my mind on either point.

I took my seat in the place appropriated to Jurors in waiting, and I looked about the Court as well as I could through the cloud of fog and breath that was heavy in it. I noticed the black vapour hanging like a murky curtain outside the great windows, and I noticed the stifled sound of wheels on the straw or tan that was littered in the street; also, the hum of the people gathered there, which a shrill whistle, or a louder song or hail than the rest, occasionally pierced. Soon afterwards the Judges, two in number, entered, and took their seats. The buzz in the Court was awfully hushed. The direction was given to put the Murderer to the bar. He appeared there. And in that same instant I recognised in him the first of the two men who had gone down Piccadilly.

If my name had been called then, I doubt if I could have answered to it audibly. But it was called about sixth or eighth in the panel, and I was by that time able to say, "Here!" Now, observe. As I stepped into the box, the prisoner, who had been looking on attentively, but with no sign of concern, became violently agitated, and beckoned to his attorney. The prisoner's wish to challenge me was so manifest, that it occasioned a pause, during which the attorney, with his hand upon the dock, whispered with his client, and shook his head. I afterwards had it from that gentleman, that the prisoner's first affrighted words to him were, "AT ALL HAZARDS, CHALLENGE THAT MAN!" But that, as he would give no reason for it, and admitted that he had not even known my name until he heard it called and I appeared, it was not done.

Both on the ground already explained, that I wish to avoid reviving the unwholesome memory of that Murderer, and also because a detailed account of his long trial is by no means indispensable to my narrative, I shall confine myself closely to such incidents in the ten days and nights during which we, the Jury, were kept together, as directly bear on my own curious personal experience. It is in that, and not in the Murderer, that I seek to interest my reader. It is to that, and not to a page of the Newgate Calendar, that I beg attention.

I was chosen Foreman of the Jury. On the second morning of the trial, after evidence had been taken for two hours (I heard the church clocks strike), happening to cast my eyes over my brother jurymen, I found an inexplicable difficulty in counting them. I counted them several times, yet always with the same difficulty. In short, I made them one too many.

I touched the brother jurymen whose place was next me, and I whispered to him, "Oblige me by counting us." He looked surprised by the request, but turned his head and counted. "Why," says he, suddenly, "we are Thirt-; but no, it's not possible. No. We are twelve."

According to my counting that day, we were always right in detail, but in the gross we were always one too many. There was no appearance, no figure, to account for it; but I had now an inward foreshadowing of the figure that was surely coming.

The Jury were housed at the London Tavern. We all slept in one large room on separate tables, and we were constantly in the charge and under the eye of the officer sworn to hold us in safe-keeping. I see no reason for suppressing the real name of that officer. He was intelligent, highly polite, and obliging, and (I was glad to hear) much respected in the City. He had an agreeable presence, good eyes, enviable black whiskers, and a fine sonorous voice. His name was Mr. Harker.

When we turned into our twelve beds at night, Mr. Harker's bed was drawn across the door. On the night of the second day, not being disposed to lie down, and seeing Mr. Harker sitting on his bed, I went and sat beside him, and offered him a pinch of snuff. As Mr. Harker's hand touched mine in taking it from my box, a peculiar shiver crossed him, and he said, "Who is this?"

Following Mr. Harker's eyes, and looking along the room, I saw again the figure I expected, the second of the two men who had gone down Piccadilly. I rose, and advanced a few steps; then stopped, and looked round at Mr. Harker. He was quite unconcerned, laughed, and said in a pleasant way, "I thought for a moment we had a thirteenth juryman, without a bed. But I see it is the moonlight."

Making no revelation to Mr. Harker, but inviting him to take a walk with me to the end of the room, I watched what the figure did. It stood for a few moments by the bedside of each of my eleven brother jurymen, close to the pillow. It always went to the right-hand side of the bed, and always passed out crossing the foot of the next bed. It seemed, from the action of the head, merely to look down pensively at each recumbent figure. It took no notice of me, or of my bed, which was that nearest to Mr. Harker's. It seemed to go out where the moonlight came in, through a high window, as by an aerial flight of stairs.

Next morning at breakfast, it appeared that everybody present had dreamed of the murdered man last night, except myself and Mr. Harker.

I now felt as convinced that the second man who had gone down Piccadilly was the murdered man (so to speak), as if it had been borne into my comprehension by his immediate testimony. But even this took place, and in a manner for which I was not at all prepared.

On the fifth day of the trial, when the case for the prosecution was drawing to a close, a miniature of the murdered man, missing from his bedroom upon the discovery of the deed, and afterwards found in a hiding-place where the Murderer had been seen digging, was put in evidence. Having been identified by the witness under examination, it was handed up to the Bench, and thence handed down to be inspected by the Jury. As an officer in a black gown was making his way with it across to me, the figure of the second man who had gone down Piccadilly impetuously started from the crowd, caught the miniature from the officer, and gave it to me with his own hands, at the same time saying, in a low and hollow tone, before I saw the miniature, which was in a locket, "I WAS YOUNGER THEN, AND MY FACE WAS NOT THEN DRAINED OF BLOOD." It also came between me and the brother juryman to whom I would have given the miniature, and between him and the brother juryman to whom he would have given it, and so passed it on through the whole of our number, and back into my possession. Not one of them, however, detected this.

At table, and generally when we were shut up together in Mr. Harker's custody, we had from the first naturally discussed the day's proceedings a good deal. On that fifth day, the case for the prosecution being closed, and we having that side of the question in a completed shape before us, our discussion was more animated and serious. Among our number was a vestryman, the densest idiot I have ever seen at large, who met the plainest evidence with the most preposterous objections, and who was sided with by two flabby parochial parasites; all the three impanelled from a district so delivered over to Fever that they ought to have been upon their own trial for five hundred Murders. When these mischievous blockheads were at their loudest, which was towards midnight, while some of us were already preparing for bed, I again saw the murdered man. He stood grimly behind them, beckoning to me. On my going towards them, and striking into the conversation, he immediately retired. This was the beginning of a separate series of appearances, confined to that long room in which we were confined. Whenever a knot of my brother jurymen laid their heads together, I saw the head of the murdered man among theirs. Whenever their comparison of notes was going against him, he would solemnly and irresistibly beckon to me.

It will be borne in mind that down to the production of the miniature, on the fifth day of the trial, I had never seen the Appearance in Court. Three changes occurred now that we entered on the case for the defence. Two of them I will mention together, first. The figure was now in Court continually, and it never there addressed itself to me, but always to the person who was speaking at the time. For instance: the throat of the murdered man had been cut straight across. In the opening speech for the defence, it was suggested that the deceased might have cut his own throat. At that very moment, the figure, with its throat in the dreadful condition referred to (this it had concealed before), stood at the speaker's elbow, motioning across and across its windpipe, now with the right hand, now with the left, vigorously suggesting to the speaker himself the impossibility of such a wound having been self-inflicted by either hand. For another instance: a witness to character, a woman, deposed to the prisoner's being the most amiable of mankind. The figure at that instant stood on the floor before her, looking her full in the face, and pointing out the prisoner's evil countenance with an extended arm and an outstretched finger.

The third change now to be added impressed me strongly as the most marked and striking of all. I do not theorise upon it; I accurately state it, and there leave it. Although the Appearance was not itself perceived by those whom it addressed, its coming close to such persons was invariably attended by some trepidation or disturbance on their part. It seemed to me as if it were prevented, by laws to which I was not amenable, from fully revealing itself to others, and yet as if it could invisibly, dumbly, and darkly overshadow their minds. When the leading counsel for the defence suggested that hypothesis of suicide, and the figure stood at the learned gentleman's elbow, frightfully sawing at its severed throat, it is undeniable that the counsel faltered in his speech, lost for a few seconds the thread of his ingenious discourse, wiped his forehead with his handkerchief, and turned extremely pale. When the witness to character was confronted by the Appearance, her eyes most certainly did follow the direction of its pointed finger, and rest in great hesitation and trouble upon the prisoner's face. Two additional illustrations will suffice. On the eighth day of the trial, after the pause which was every day made early in the afternoon for a few minutes' rest and refreshment, I came back into Court with the rest of the Jury some little time before the return of the Judges. Standing up in the box and looking about me, I thought the figure was not there, until, chancing to raise my eyes to the gallery, I saw it bending forward, and leaning over a very decent woman, as if to assure itself whether the Judges had resumed their seats or not. Immediately afterwards that woman screamed, fainted, and was carried out. So with the venerable, sagacious, and patient Judge who conducted the trial. When the case was over, and he settled himself and his papers to sum up, the murdered man, entering by the Judges' door, advanced to his Lordship's desk, and looked eagerly over his shoulder at the pages of his notes which he was turning. A change came over his Lordship's face; his hand stopped; the peculiar shiver, that I knew so well, passed over him; he faltered, "Excuse me, gentlemen, for a few moments. I am somewhat oppressed by the vitiated air;" and did not recover until he had drunk a glass of water.

Through all the monotony of six of those interminable ten days, the same Judges and others on the bench, the same Murderer in the dock, the same lawyers at the table, the same tones of question and answer rising to the roof of the court, the same scratching of the Judge's pen, the same ushers going in and out, the same lights kindled at the same hour when there had been any natural light of day, the same foggy curtain outside the great windows when it was foggy, the same rain pattering and dripping when it was rainy, the same footmarks of turnkeys and prisoner day after day on the same sawdust, the same keys locking and unlocking the same heavy doors, through all the wearisome monotony which made me feel as if I had been Foreman of the Jury for a vast cried of time, and Piccadilly had flourished coevally with Babylon, the murdered man never lost one trace of his distinctness in my eyes, nor was he at any moment less distinct than anybody else. I must not omit, as a matter of fact, that I never once saw the Appearance which I call by the name of the murdered man look at the Murderer. Again and again I wondered, "Why does he not?" But he never did.

Nor did he look at me, after the production of the miniature, until the last closing minutes of the trial arrived. We retired to consider, at seven minutes before ten at night. The idiotic vestryman and his two parochial parasites gave us so much trouble that we twice returned into Court to beg to have certain extracts from the Judge's notes re-read. Nine of us had not the smallest doubt about those passages, neither,

I believe, had any one in the Court; the dunder-headed triumvirate, having no idea but obstruction, disputed them for that very reason. At length we prevailed, and finally the Jury returned into Court at ten minutes past twelve.

The murdered man at that time stood directly opposite the Jury-box, on the other side of the Court. As I took my place, his eyes rested on me with great attention; he seemed satisfied, and slowly shook a great gray veil, which he carried on his arm for the first time, over his head and whole form. As I gave in our verdict, "Guilty," the veil collapsed, all was gone, and his place was empty.

The Murderer, being asked by the Judge, according to usage, whether he had anything to say before sentence of Death should be passed upon him, indistinctly muttered something which was described in the leading newspapers of the following day as "a few rambling, incoherent, and half-audible words, in which he was understood to complain that he had not had a fair trial, because the Foreman of the Jury was prepossessed against him." The remarkable declaration that he really made was this: "MY LORD, I KNEW I WAS A DOOMED MAN, WHEN THE FOREMAN OF MY JURY CAME INTO THE BOX. MY LORD, I KNEW HE WOULD NEVER LET ME OFF, BECAUSE, BEFORE I WAS TAKEN, HE SOMEHOW GOT TO MY BEDSIDE IN THE NIGHT, WOKE ME, AND PUT A ROPE ROUND MY NECK."

Hunted Down

Most of us see some romances in life. In my capacity as Chief Manager of a Life Assurance Office, I think I have within the last thirty years seen more romances than the generality of men, however unpromising the opportunity may, at first sight, seem.

As I have retired, and live at my ease, I possess the means that I used to want, of considering what I have seen, at leisure. My experiences have a more remarkable aspect, so reviewed, than they had when they were in progress. I have come home from the Play now, and can recall the scenes of the Drama upon which the curtain has fallen, free from the glare, bewilderment, and bustle of the Theatre.

Let me recall one of these Romances of the real world.

There is nothing truer than physiognomy, taken in connection with manner. The art of reading that book of which Eternal Wisdom obliges every human creature to present his or her own page with the individual character written on it, is a difficult one, perhaps, and is little studied. It may require some natural aptitude, and it must require (for everything does) some patience and some pains. That these are not usually given to it, - that numbers of people accept a few stock commonplace expressions of the face as the whole list of characteristics, and neither seek nor know the refinements that are truest, - that You, for instance, give a great deal of time and attention to the reading of music, Greek, Latin, French, Italian, Hebrew, if you please, and do not qualify yourself to read the face of the master or mistress looking over your shoulder teaching it to you, - I assume to be five hundred times more probable than improbable. Perhaps a little self-sufficiency may be at the bottom of this; facial expression requires no study from you, you think; it comes by nature to you to know enough about it, and you are not to be taken in.

I confess, for my part, that I HAVE been taken in, over and over again. I have been taken in by acquaintances, and I have been taken in (of course) by friends; far oftener by friends than by any other class of persons. How came I to be so deceived? Had I quite misread their faces?

No. Believe me, my first impression of those people, founded on face and manner alone, was invariably true. My mistake was in suffering them to come nearer to me and explain themselves away.

The partition which separated my own office from our general outer office in the City was of thick plate-glass. I could see through it what passed in the outer office, without hearing a word. I had it put up in place of a wall that had been there for years, - ever since the house was built. It is no matter whether I did or did not make the change in order that I might derive my first impression of strangers, who came to us on business, from their faces alone, without being influenced by anything they said. Enough to mention that I turned my glass partition to that account, and that a Life Assurance Office is at all times exposed to be practised upon by the most crafty and cruel of the human race.

It was through my glass partition that I first saw the gentleman whose story I am going to tell.

He had come in without my observing it, and had put his hat and umbrella on the broad counter, and was bending over it to take some papers from one of the clerks. He was about forty or so, dark, exceedingly well dressed in black, - being in mourning, - and the hand he extended with a polite air, had a particularly well-fitting black-kid glove upon it. His hair, which was elaborately brushed and oiled, was parted straight up the middle; and he presented this parting to the clerk, exactly (to my thinking) as if he had said, in so many words: 'You must take me, if you please, my friend, just as I show myself. Come straight up here, follow the gravel path, keep off the grass, I allow no trespassing.'

I conceived a very great aversion to that man the moment I thus saw him.

He had asked for some of our printed forms, and the clerk was giving them to him and explaining them. An obliged and agreeable smile was on his face, and his eyes met those of the clerk with a sprightly look. (I have known a vast quantity of nonsense talked about bad men not looking you in the face. Don't trust that conventional idea. Dishonesty will stare honesty out of countenance, any day in the week, if there is anything to be got by it.)

I saw, in the corner of his eyelash, that he became aware of my looking at him. Immediately he turned the parting in his hair toward the glass partition, as if he said to me with a sweet smile, 'Straight up here, if you please. Off the grass!'

In a few moments he had put on his hat and taken up his umbrella, and was gone.

I beckoned the clerk into my room, and asked, 'Who was that?'

He had the gentleman's card in his hand. 'Mr. Julius Slinkton, Middle Temple.'

'A barrister, Mr. Adams?'

'I think not, sir.'

'I should have thought him a clergyman, but for his having no Reverend here,' said I.

'Probably, from his appearance,' Mr. Adams replied, 'he is reading for orders.'

I should mention that he wore a dainty white cravat, and dainty linen altogether.

'What did he want, Mr. Adams?'

'Merely a form of proposal, sir, and form of reference.'

'Recommended here? Did he say?'

'Yes, he said he was recommended here by a friend of yours. He noticed you, but said that as he had not the pleasure of your personal acquaintance he would not trouble you.'

'Did he know my name?'

'O yes, sir! He said, "There IS Mr. Sampson, I see!"'

'A well-spoken gentleman, apparently?'

'Remarkably so, sir.'

'Insinuating manners, apparently?'

'Very much so, indeed, sir.'

'Hah!' said I. 'I want nothing at present, Mr. Adams.'

Within a fortnight of that day I went to dine with a friend of mine, a merchant, a man of taste, who buys pictures and books, and the first man I saw among the company was Mr. Julius Slinkton. There he was, standing before the fire, with good large eyes and an open expression of face; but still (I thought) requiring everybody to come at him by the prepared way he offered, and by no other.

I noticed him ask my friend to introduce him to Mr. Sampson, and my friend did so. Mr. Slinkton was very happy to see me. Not too happy; there was no over-doing of the matter; happy in a thoroughly well-bred, perfectly unmeaning way.

'I thought you had met,' our host observed.

'No,' said Mr. Slinkton. 'I did look in at Mr. Sampson's office, on your recommendation; but I really did not feel justified in troubling Mr. Sampson himself, on a point in the everyday, routine of an ordinary clerk.'

I said I should have been glad to show him any attention on our friend's introduction.

'I am sure of that,' said he, 'and am much obliged. At another time, perhaps, I may be less delicate. Only, however, if I have real business; for I know, Mr. Sampson, how precious business time is, and what a vast number of impertinent people there are in the world.'

I acknowledged his consideration with a slight bow. 'You were thinking,' said I, 'of effecting a policy on your life.'

'O dear no! I am afraid I am not so prudent as you pay me the compliment of supposing me to be, Mr. Sampson. I merely inquired for a friend. But you know what friends are in such matters. Nothing may ever come of it. I have the greatest reluctance to trouble men of business with inquiries for friends, knowing the probabilities to be a thousand to one that the friends will never follow them up. People are so fickle, so selfish, so inconsiderate. Don't you, in your business, find them so every day, Mr. Sampson?'

I was going to give a qualified answer; but he turned his smooth, white parting on me with its 'Straight up here, if you please!' and I answered 'Yes.'

'I hear, Mr. Sampson,' he resumed presently, for our friend had a new cook, and dinner was not so punctual as usual, 'that your profession has recently suffered a great loss.'

'In money?' said I.

He laughed at my ready association of loss with money, and replied, 'No, in talent and vigour.'

Not at once following out his allusion, I considered for a moment. 'HAS it sustained a loss of that kind?' said I. 'I was not aware of it.'

'Understand me, Mr. Sampson. I don't imagine that you have retired. It is not so bad as that. But Mr. Meltham - '

'O, to be sure!' said I. 'Yes! Mr. Meltham, the young actuary of the "Inestimable."'

'Just so,' he returned in a consoling way.

'He is a great loss. He was at once the most profound, the most original, and the most energetic man I have ever known connected with Life Assurance.'

I spoke strongly; for I had a high esteem and admiration for Meltham; and my gentleman had indefinitely conveyed to me some suspicion that he wanted to sneer at him. He recalled me to my guard by presenting that trim pathway up his head, with its internal 'Not on the grass, if you please - the gravel.'

'You knew him, Mr. Slinkton.'

'Only by reputation. To have known him as an acquaintance or as a friend, is an honour I should have sought if he had remained in society, though I might never have had the good fortune to attain it, being a man of far inferior mark. He was scarcely above thirty, I suppose?'

'About thirty.'

'Ah!' he sighed in his former consoling way. 'What creatures we are! To break up, Mr. Sampson, and become incapable of business at that time of life! - Any reason assigned for the melancholy fact?'

('Humph!' thought I, as I looked at him. 'But I WON'T go up the track, and I WILL go on the grass.')

'What reason have you heard assigned, Mr. Slinkton?' I asked, point-blank.

'Most likely a false one. You know what Rumour is, Mr. Sampson. I never repeat what I hear; it is the only way of paring the nails and shaving the head of Rumour. But when YOU ask me what reason I have heard assigned for Mr. Meltham's passing away from among men, it is another thing. I am not gratifying idle gossip then. I was told, Mr. Sampson, that Mr. Meltham had relinquished all his avocations and all his prospects, because he was, in fact, broken-hearted. A disappointed attachment I heard, - though it hardly seems probable, in the case of a man so distinguished and so attractive.'

'Attractions and distinctions are no armour against death,' said I.

'O, she died? Pray pardon me. I did not hear that. That, indeed, makes it very, very sad. Poor Mr. Meltham! She died? Ah, dear me! Lamentable, lamentable!'

I still thought his pity was not quite genuine, and I still suspected an unaccountable sneer under all this, until he said, as we were parted, like the other knots of talkers, by the announcement of dinner:

'Mr. Sampson, you are surprised to see me so moved on behalf of a man whom I have never known. I am not so disinterested as you may suppose. I have suffered, and recently too, from death myself. I have lost one of two charming nieces, who were my constant companions. She died young - barely three-and-twenty; and even her remaining sister is far from strong. The world is a grave!'

He said this with deep feeling, and I felt reproached for the coldness of my manner. Coldness and distrust had been engendered in me, I knew, by my bad experiences; they were not natural to me; and I often thought how much I had lost in life, losing trustfulness, and how little I had gained, gaining hard caution. This state of mind being habitual to me, I troubled myself more about this conversation than I might have troubled myself about a greater matter. I listened to his talk at dinner, and observed how readily other men responded to it, and with what a graceful instinct he adapted his subjects to the knowledge and habits of those he talked with. As, in talking with me, he had easily started the subject I might be supposed to understand best, and to be the most interested in, so, in talking with others, he guided himself by the same rule. The company was of a varied character; but he was not at fault, that I could discover, with any member of it. He knew just as much of each man's pursuit as made him agreeable to that man in reference to it, and just as little as made it natural in him to seek modestly for information when the theme was broached.

As he talked and talked - but really not too much, for the rest of us seemed to force it upon him - I became quite angry with myself. I took his face to pieces in my mind, like a watch, and examined it in detail. I could not say much against any of his features separately; I could say even less against them when they were put together. 'Then is it not monstrous,' I asked myself, 'that because a man happens to part his hair straight up the middle of his head, I should permit myself to suspect, and even to detest him?'

(I may stop to remark that this was no proof of my sense. An observer of men who finds himself steadily repelled by some apparently trifling thing in a stranger is right to give it great weight. It may be the clue to the whole mystery. A hair or two will show where a lion is hidden. A very little key will open a very heavy door.)

I took my part in the conversation with him after a time, and we got on remarkably well. In the drawing-room I asked the host how long he had known Mr. Slinkton. He answered, not many months; he had met him at the house of a celebrated painter then present, who had known him well when he was travelling with his nieces in Italy for their health. His plans in life being broken by the death of one of them, he was reading with the intention of going back to college as a matter of form, taking his degree, and going into orders. I could not but argue with myself that here was the true explanation of his interest in poor Meltham, and that I had been almost brutal in my distrust on that simple head.

On the very next day but one I was sitting behind my glass partition, as before, when he came into the outer office, as before. The moment I saw him again without hearing him, I hated him worse than ever.

It was only for a moment that I had this opportunity; for he waved his tight-fitting black glove the instant I looked at him, and came straight in.

'Mr. Sampson, good-day! I presume, you see, upon your kind permission to intrude upon you. I don't keep my word in being justified by business, for my business here - if I may so abuse the word - is of the slightest nature.'

I asked, was it anything I could assist him in?

'I thank you, no. I merely called to inquire outside whether my dilatory friend had been so false to himself as to be practical and sensible. But, of course, he has done nothing. I gave him your papers with my own hand, and he was hot upon the intention, but of course he has done nothing. Apart from the general human disinclination to do anything that ought to be done, I dare say there is a specially about assuring one's life. You find it like will-making. People are so superstitious, and take it for granted they will die soon afterwards.'

'Up here, if you please; straight up here, Mr. Sampson. Neither to the right nor to the left.' I almost fancied I could hear him breathe the words as he sat smiling at me, with that intolerable parting exactly opposite the bridge of my nose.

'There is such a feeling sometimes, no doubt,' I replied; 'but I don't think it obtains to any great extent.'

'Well,' said he, with a shrug and a smile, 'I wish some good angel would influence my friend in the right direction. I rashly promised his mother and sister in Norfolk to see it done, and he promised them that he would do it. But I suppose he never will.'

He spoke for a minute or two on indifferent topics, and went away.

I had scarcely unlocked the drawers of my writing-table next morning, when he reappeared. I noticed that he came straight to the door in the glass partition, and did not pause a single moment outside.

'Can you spare me two minutes, my dear Mr. Sampson?'

'By all means.'

'Much obliged,' laying his hat and umbrella on the table; 'I came early, not to interrupt you. The fact is, I am taken by surprise in reference to this proposal my friend has made.'

'Has he made one?' said I.

'Ye-es,' he answered, deliberately looking at me; and then a bright idea seemed to strike him - 'or he only tells me he has. Perhaps that may be a new way of evading the matter. By Jupiter, I never thought of that!'

Mr. Adams was opening the morning's letters in the outer office. 'What is the name, Mr. Slinkton?' I asked.

'Beckwith.'

I looked out at the door and requested Mr. Adams, if there were a proposal in that name, to bring it in. He had already laid it out of his hand on the counter. It was easily selected from the rest, and he gave it me. Alfred Beckwith. Proposal to effect a policy with us for two thousand pounds. Dated yesterday.

'From the Middle Temple, I see, Mr. Slinkton.'

'Yes. He lives on the same staircase with me; his door is opposite. I never thought he would make me his reference though.'

'It seems natural enough that he should.'

'Quite so, Mr. Sampson; but I never thought of it. Let me see.' He took the printed paper from his pocket. 'How am I to answer all these questions?'

'According to the truth, of course,' said I.

'O, of course!' he answered, looking up from the paper with a smile; 'I meant they were so many. But you do right to be particular. It stands to reason that you must be particular. Will you allow me to use your pen and ink?'

'Certainly.'

'And your desk?'

'Certainly.'

He had been hovering about between his hat and his umbrella for a place to write on. He now sat down in my chair, at my blotting-paper and inkstand, with the long walk up his head in accurate perspective before me, as I stood with my back to the fire.

Before answering each question he ran over it aloud, and discussed it. How long had he known Mr. Alfred Beckwith? That he had to calculate by years upon his fingers. What were his habits? No difficulty about them; temperate in the last degree, and took a little too much exercise, if anything. All the answers were satisfactory. When he had written them all, he looked them over, and finally signed them in a very pretty hand. He supposed he had now done with the business. I told him he was not likely to be troubled any farther. Should he leave the papers there? If he pleased. Much obliged. Good-morning.

I had had one other visitor before him; not at the office, but at my own house. That visitor had come to my bedside when it was not yet daylight, and had been seen by no one else but by my faithful confidential servant.

A second reference paper (for we required always two) was sent down into Norfolk, and was duly received back by post. This, likewise, was satisfactorily answered in every respect. Our forms were all complied with; we accepted the proposal, and the premium for one year was paid.

For six or seven months I saw no more of Mr. Slinkton. He called once at my house, but I was not at home; and he once asked me to dine with him in the Temple, but I was engaged. His friend's assurance was effected in March. Late in September or early in October I was down at Scarborough for a breath of sea-air, where I met him on the beach. It was a hot evening; he came toward me with his hat in his hand; and there was the walk I had felt so strongly disinclined to take in perfect order again, exactly in front of the bridge of my nose.

He was not alone, but had a young lady on his arm.

She was dressed in mourning, and I looked at her with great interest. She had the appearance of being extremely delicate, and her face was remarkably pale and melancholy; but she was very pretty. He introduced her as his niece, Miss Niner.

'Are you strolling, Mr. Sampson? Is it possible you can be idle?'

It WAS possible, and I WAS strolling.

'Shall we stroll together?'

'With pleasure.'

The young lady walked between us, and we walked on the cool sea sand, in the direction of Filey.

'There have been wheels here,' said Mr. Slinkton. 'And now I look again, the wheels of a hand-carriage! Margaret, my love, your shadow without doubt!'

'Miss Niner's shadow?' I repeated, looking down at it on the sand.

'Not that one,' Mr. Slinkton returned, laughing. 'Margaret, my dear, tell Mr. Sampson.'

'Indeed,' said the young lady, turning to me, 'there is nothing to tell - except that I constantly see the same invalid old gentleman at all times, wherever I go. I have mentioned it to my uncle, and he calls the gentleman my shadow.'

'Does he live in Scarborough?' I asked.

'He is staying here.'

'Do you live in Scarborough?'

'No, I am staying here. My uncle has placed me with a family here, for my health.'

'And your shadow?' said I, smiling.

'My shadow,' she answered, smiling too, 'is - like myself – not very robust, I fear; for I lose my shadow sometimes, as my shadow loses me at other times. We both seem liable to confinement to the house. I have not seen my shadow for days and days; but it does oddly happen, occasionally, that wherever I go, for many days together, this gentleman goes. We have come together in the most unfrequented nooks on this shore.'

'Is this he?' said I, pointing before us.

The wheels had swept down to the water's edge, and described a great loop on the sand in turning. Bringing the loop back towards us, and spinning it out as it came, was a hand-carriage, drawn by a man.

'Yes,' said Miss Niner, 'this really is my shadow, uncle.'

As the carriage approached us and we approached the carriage, I saw within it an old man, whose head was sunk on his breast, and who was enveloped in a variety of wrappers. He was drawn by a very quiet but very keen-looking man, with iron-gray hair, who was slightly lame. They had passed us, when the carriage stopped, and the old gentleman within, putting out his arm, called to me by my name. I went back, and was absent from Mr. Slinkton and his niece for about five minutes.

When I rejoined them, Mr. Slinkton was the first to speak. Indeed, he said to me in a raised voice before I came up with him:

'It is well you have not been longer, or my niece might have died of curiosity to know who her shadow is, Mr. Sampson.'

'An old East India Director,' said I. 'An intimate friend of our friend's, at whose house I first had the pleasure of meeting you. A certain Major Banks. You have heard of him?'

'Never.'

'Very rich, Miss Niner; but very old, and very crippled. An amiable man, sensible - much interested in you. He has just been expatiating on the affection that he has observed to exist between you and your uncle.'

Mr. Slinkton was holding his hat again, and he passed his hand up the straight walk, as if he himself went up it serenely, after me.

'Mr. Sampson,' he said, tenderly pressing his niece's arm in his, 'our affection was always a strong one, for we have had but few near ties. We have still fewer now. We have associations to bring us together, that are not of this world, Margaret.'

'Dear uncle!' murmured the young lady, and turned her face aside to hide her tears.

'My niece and I have such remembrances and regrets in common, Mr. Sampson,' he feelingly pursued, 'that it would be strange indeed if the relations between us were cold or indifferent. If I remember a conversation we once had together, you will understand the reference I make. Cheer up, dear Margaret. Don't droop, don't droop. My Margaret! I cannot bear to see you droop!'

The poor young lady was very much affected, but controlled herself. His feelings, too, were very acute. In a word, he found himself under such great need of a restorative, that he presently went away, to take a bath of sea-water, leaving the young lady and me sitting by a point of rock, and probably presuming - but that you will say was a pardonable indulgence in a luxury - that she would praise him with all her heart.

She did, poor thing! With all her confiding heart, she praised him to me, for his care of her dead sister, and for his untiring devotion in her last illness. The sister had wasted away very slowly, and wild and terrible fantasies had come over her toward the end, but he had never been impatient with her, or at a loss; had always been gentle, watchful, and self-possessed. The sister had known him, as she had known him, to be the best of men, the kindest of men, and yet a man of such admirable strength of character, as to be a very tower for the support of their weak natures while their poor lives endured.

'I shall leave him, Mr. Sampson, very soon,' said the young lady; 'I know my life is drawing to an end; and when I am gone, I hope he will marry and be happy. I am sure he has lived single so long, only for my sake, and for my poor, poor sister's.'

The little hand-carriage had made another great loop on the damp sand, and was coming back again, gradually spinning out a slim figure of eight, half a mile long.

'Young lady,' said I, looking around, laying my hand upon her arm, and speaking in a low voice, 'time presses. You hear the gentle murmur of that sea?'

She looked at me with the utmost wonder and alarm, saying, 'Yes!'

'And you know what a voice is in it when the storm comes?'

'Yes!'

'You see how quiet and peaceful it lies before us, and you know what an awful sight of power without pity it might be, this very night!'

'Yes!'

'But if you had never heard or seen it, or heard of it in its cruelty, could you believe that it beats every inanimate thing in its way to pieces, without mercy, and destroys life without remorse?'

'You terrify me, sir, by these questions!'

'To save you, young lady, to save you! For God's sake, collect your strength and collect your firmness! If you were here alone, and hemmed in by the rising tide on the flow to fifty feet above your head, you could not be in greater danger than the danger you are now to be saved from.'

The figure on the sand was spun out, and straggled off into a crooked little jerk that ended at the cliff very near us.

'As I am, before Heaven and the Judge of all mankind, your friend, and your dead sister's friend, I solemnly entreat you, Miss Niner, without one moment's loss of time, to come to this gentleman with me!'

If the little carriage had been less near to us, I doubt if I could have got her away; but it was so near that we were there before she had recovered the hurry of being urged from the rock. I did not remain there with her two minutes. Certainly within five, I had the inexpressible satisfaction of seeing her - from the point we had sat on, and to which I had returned - half supported and half carried up some rude steps notched in the cliff, by the figure of an active man. With that figure beside her, I knew she was safe anywhere.

I sat alone on the rock, awaiting Mr. Slinkton's return. The twilight was deepening and the shadows were heavy, when he came round the point, with his hat hanging at his button-hole, smoothing his wet hair with one of his hands, and picking out the old path with the other and a pocket-comb.

'My niece not here, Mr. Sampson?' he said, looking about.

'Miss Niner seemed to feel a chill in the air after the sun was down, and has gone home.'

He looked surprised, as though she were not accustomed to do anything without him; even to originate so slight a proceeding.

'I persuaded Miss Niner,' I explained.

'Ah!' said he. 'She is easily persuaded - for her good. Thank you, Mr. Sampson; she is better within doors. The bathing-place was farther than I thought, to say the truth.'

'Miss Niner is very delicate,' I observed.

He shook his head and drew a deep sigh. 'Very, very, very. You may recollect my saying so. The time that has since intervened has not strengthened her. The gloomy shadow that fell upon her sister so early in life seems, in my anxious eyes, to gather over her, ever darker, ever darker. Dear Margaret, dear Margaret! But we must hope.'

The hand-carriage was spinning away before us at a most indecorous pace for an invalid vehicle, and was making most irregular curves upon the sand. Mr. Slinkton, noticing it after he had put his handkerchief to his eyes, said;

'If I may judge from appearances, your friend will be upset, Mr. Sampson.'

'It looks probable, certainly,' said I.

'The servant must be drunk.'

'The servants of old gentlemen will get drunk sometimes,' said I.

'The major draws very light, Mr. Sampson.'

'The major does draw light,' said I.

By this time the carriage, much to my relief, was lost in the darkness. We walked on for a little, side by side over the sand, in silence. After a short while he said, in a voice still affected by the emotion that his niece's state of health had awakened in him,

'Do you stay here long, Mr. Sampson?'

'Why, no. I am going away to-night.'

'So soon? But business always holds you in request. Men like Mr. Sampson are too important to others, to be spared to their own need of relaxation and enjoyment.'

'I don't know about that,' said I. 'However, I am going back.'

'To London?'

'To London.'

'I shall be there too, soon after you.'

I knew that as well as he did. But I did not tell him so. Any more than I told him what defensive weapon my right hand rested on in my pocket, as I walked by his side. Any more than I told him why I did not walk on the sea side of him with the night closing in.

We left the beach, and our ways diverged. We exchanged goodnight, and had parted indeed, when he said, returning,

'Mr. Sampson, MAY I ask? Poor Meltham, whom we spoke of, - dead yet?'

'Not when I last heard of him; but too broken a man to live long, and hopelessly lost to his old calling.'

'Dear, dear, dear!' said he, with great feeling. 'Sad, sad, sad! The world is a grave!' And so went his way.

It was not his fault if the world were not a grave; but I did not call that observation after him, any more than I had mentioned those other things just now enumerated. He went his way, and I went mine with all expedition. This happened, as I have said, either at the end of September or beginning of October. The next time I saw him, and the last time, was late in November.

I had a very particular engagement to breakfast in the Temple. It was a bitter north-easterly morning, and the sleet and slush lay inches deep in the streets. I could get no conveyance, and was soon wet to the knees; but I should have been true to that appointment, though I had to wade to it up to my neck in the same impediments.

The appointment took me to some chambers in the Temple. They were at the top of a lonely corner house overlooking the river. The name, MR. ALFRED BECKWITH, was painted on the outer door. On the door opposite, on the same landing, the name MR. JULIUS SLINKTON. The doors of both sets of chambers stood open, so that anything said aloud in one set could be heard in the other.

I had never been in those chambers before. They were dismal, close, unwholesome, and oppressive; the furniture, originally good, and not yet old, was faded and dirty, - the rooms were in great disorder; there was a strong prevailing smell of opium, brandy, and tobacco; the grate and fire-irons were splashed all over with unsightly blotches of rust; and on a sofa by the fire, in the room where breakfast had been prepared, lay the host, Mr. Beckwith, a man with all the appearances of the worst kind of drunkard, very far advanced upon his shameful way to death.

'Slinkton is not come yet,' said this creature, staggering up when I went in; 'I'll call him. - Halloa! Julius Caesar! Come and drink!' As he hoarsely roared this out, he beat the poker and tongs together in a mad way, as if that were his usual manner of summoning his associate.

The voice of Mr. Slinkton was heard through the clatter from the opposite side of the staircase, and he came in. He had not expected the pleasure of meeting me. I have seen several artful men brought to a stand, but I never saw a man so aghast as he was when his eyes rested on mine.

'Julius Caesar,' cried Beckwith, staggering between us, 'Mist' Sampson! Mist' Sampson, Julius Caesar! Julius, Mist' Sampson, is the friend of my soul. Julius keeps me plied with liquor, morning, noon, and night. Julius is a real benefactor. Julius threw the tea and coffee out of window when I used to have any. Julius empties all the water-jugs of their contents, and fills 'em with spirits. Julius winds me up and keeps me going. - Boil the brandy, Julius!'

There was a rusty and furred saucepan in the ashes, - the ashes looked like the accumulation of weeks, - and Beckwith, rolling and staggering between us as if he were going to plunge headlong into the fire, got the saucepan out, and tried to force it into Slinkton's hand.

'Boil the brandy, Julius Caesar! Come! Do your usual office. Boil the brandy!'

He became so fierce in his gesticulations with the saucepan, that I expected to see him lay open Slinkton's head with it. I therefore put out my hand to check him. He reeled back to the sofa, and sat there panting, shaking, and red-eyed, in his rags of dressing-gown, looking at us both. I noticed then that there was nothing to drink on the table but brandy, and nothing to eat but salted herrings, and a hot, sickly, highly-peppered stew.

'At all events, Mr. Sampson,' said Slinkton, offering me the smooth gravel path for the last time, 'I thank you for interfering between me and this unfortunate man's violence. However you came here, Mr. Sampson, or with whatever motive you came here, at least I thank you for that.'

'Boil the brandy,' muttered Beckwith.

Without gratifying his desire to know how I came there, I said, quietly, 'How is your niece, Mr. Slinkton?'

He looked hard at me, and I looked hard at him.

'I am sorry to say, Mr. Sampson, that my niece has proved treacherous and ungrateful to her best friend. She left me without a word of notice or explanation. She was misled, no doubt, by some designing rascal. Perhaps you may have heard of it.'

'I did hear that she was misled by a designing rascal. In fact, I have proof of it.'

'Are you sure of that?' said he.

'Quite.'

'Boil the brandy,' muttered Beckwith. 'Company to breakfast, Julius Caesar. Do your usual office, - provide the usual breakfast, dinner, tea, and supper. Boil the brandy!'

The eyes of Slinkton looked from him to me, and he said, after a moment's consideration,

'Mr. Sampson, you are a man of the world, and so am I. I will be plain with you.'

'O no, you won't,' said I, shaking my head.

'I tell you, sir, I will be plain with you.'

'And I tell you you will not,' said I. 'I know all about you. YOU plain with any one? Nonsense, nonsense!'

'I plainly tell you, Mr. Sampson,' he went on, with a manner almost composed, 'that I understand your object. You want to save your funds, and escape from your liabilities; these are old tricks of trade with you Office-gentlemen. But you will not do it, sir; you will not succeed. You have not an easy adversary to play against, when you play against me. We shall have to inquire, in due time, when and how Mr. Beckwith fell into his present habits. With that remark, sir, I put this poor creature, and his incoherent wanderings of speech, aside, and wish you a good morning and a better case next time.'

While he was saying this, Beckwith had filled a half-pint glass with brandy. At this moment, he threw the brandy at his face, and threw the glass after it. Slinkton put his hands up, half blinded with the spirit, and cut with the glass across the forehead. At the sound of the breakage, a fourth person came into the room, closed the door, and stood at it; he was a very quiet but very keen-looking man, with iron-gray hair, and slightly lame.

Slinkton pulled out his handkerchief, assuaged the pain in his smarting eyes, and dabbled the blood on his forehead. He was a long time about it, and I saw that in the doing of it, a tremendous change came over him, occasioned by the change in Beckwith, - who ceased to pant and tremble, sat upright, and never took his eyes off him. I never in my life saw a face in which abhorrence and determination were so forcibly painted as in Beckwith's then.

'Look at me, you villain,' said Beckwith, 'and see me as I really am. I took these rooms, to make them a trap for you. I came into them as a drunkard, to bait the trap for you. You fell into the trap, and you will never leave it alive. On the morning when you last went to Mr. Sampson's office, I had seen him first. Your plot has been known to both of us, all along, and you have been counter-plotted all along. What? Having been cajoled into putting that prize of two thousand pounds in your power, I was to be done to death with brandy, and, brandy not proving quick enough, with something quicker? Have I never seen you, when you thought my senses gone, pouring from your little bottle into my glass? Why, you Murderer and Forger, alone here with you in the dead of night, as I have so often been, I have had my hand upon the trigger of a pistol, twenty times, to blow your brains out!'

This sudden starting up of the thing that he had supposed to be his imbecile victim into a determined man, with a settled resolution to hunt him down and be the death of him, mercilessly expressed from head to foot, was, in the first shock, too much for him. Without any figure of speech, he staggered under it. But there is no greater mistake than to suppose that a man who is a calculating criminal, is, in any phase of his guilt, otherwise than true to himself, and perfectly consistent with his whole character. Such a man commits murder, and murder is the natural culmination of his course; such a man has to outface murder, and will do it with hardihood and effrontery. It is a sort of fashion to express surprise that any notorious criminal, having such crime upon his conscience, can so brave it out. Do you think that if he had it on his conscience at all, or had a conscience to have it upon, he would ever have committed the crime?

Perfectly consistent with himself, as I believe all such monsters to be, this Slinkton recovered himself, and showed a defiance that was sufficiently cold and quiet. He was white, he was haggard, he was changed; but only as a sharper who had played for a great stake and had been outwitted and had lost the game.

'Listen to me, you villain,' said Beckwith, 'and let every word you hear me say be a stab in your wicked heart. When I took these rooms, to throw myself in your way and lead you on to the scheme that I knew my appearance and supposed character and habits would suggest to such a devil, how did I know that? Because you were no stranger to me. I knew you well. And I knew you to be the cruel wretch who, for so much money, had killed one innocent girl while she trusted him implicitly, and who was by inches killing another.'

Slinkton took out a snuff-box, took a pinch of snuff, and laughed.

'But see here,' said Beckwith, never looking away, never raising his voice, never relaxing his face, never unclenching his hand. 'See what a dull wolf you have been, after all! The infatuated drunkard who never drank a fiftieth part of the liquor you plied him with, but poured it away, here, there, everywhere – almost before your eyes; who bought over the fellow you set to watch him and to ply him, by outbidding you in his bribe, before he had been at his work three days - with whom you have observed no caution, yet who was so bent on ridding the earth of you as a wild beast, that he would have defeated you if you had been ever so prudent - that drunkard whom you have, many a time, left on the floor of this room, and who has even let you go out of it, alive and undeceived, when you have turned him over with your foot - has, almost as often, on the same night, within an hour, within a few minutes, watched you awake, had his hand at your pillow when you were asleep, turned over your papers, taken samples from your bottles and packets of powder, changed their contents, rifled every secret of your life!'

He had had another pinch of snuff in his hand, but had gradually let it drop from between his fingers to the floor; where he now smoothed it out with his foot, looking down at it the while.

'That drunkard,' said Beckwith, 'who had free access to your rooms at all times, that he might drink the strong drinks that you left in his way and be the sooner ended, holding no more terms with you than he would hold with a tiger, has had his master-key for all your locks, his test for all your poisons, his clue to your cipher-writing. He can tell you, as well as you can tell him, how long it took to complete that deed, what doses there were, what intervals, what signs of gradual decay upon mind and body; what distempered fancies were produced, what observable changes, what physical pain. He can tell you, as well as you can tell him, that all this was recorded day by day, as a lesson of experience for future service. He can tell you, better than you can tell him, where that journal is at this moment.'

Slinkton stopped the action of his foot, and looked at Beckwith.

'No,' said the latter, as if answering a question from him. 'Not in the drawer of the writing-desk that opens with a spring; it is not there, and it never will be there again.'

'Then you are a thief!' said Slinkton.

Without any change whatever in the inflexible purpose, which it was quite terrific even to me to contemplate, and from the power of which I had always felt convinced it was impossible for this wretch to escape, Beckwith returned,

'And I am your niece's shadow, too.'

With an imprecation Slinkton put his hand to his head, tore out some hair, and flung it to the ground. It was the end of the smooth walk; he destroyed it in the action, and it will soon be seen that his use for it was past.

Beckwith went on: 'Whenever you left here, I left here. Although I understood that you found it necessary to pause in the completion of that purpose, to avert suspicion, still I watched you close, with the poor confiding girl. When I had the diary, and could read it word by word, - it was only about the night before your last visit to Scarborough, - you remember the night? you slept with a small flat vial tied to your wrist, - I sent to Mr. Sampson, who was kept out of view. This is Mr. Sampson's trusty servant standing by the door. We three saved your niece among us.'

Slinkton looked at us all, took an uncertain step or two from the place where he had stood, returned to it, and glanced about him in a very curious way, - as one of the meaner reptiles might, looking for a hole to hide in. I noticed at the same time, that a singular change took place in the figure of the man, - as if it collapsed within his clothes, and they consequently became ill-shaped and ill-fitting.

'You shall know,' said Beckwith, 'for I hope the knowledge will be bitter and terrible to you, why you have been pursued by one man, and why, when the whole interest that Mr. Sampson represents would have expended any money in hunting you down, you have been tracked to death at a single individual's charge. I hear you have had the name of Meltham on your lips sometimes?'

I saw, in addition to those other changes, a sudden stoppage come upon his breathing.

'When you sent the sweet girl whom you murdered (you know with what artfully made-out surroundings and probabilities you sent her) to Meltham's office, before taking her abroad to originate the transaction that doomed her to the grave, it fell to Meltham's lot to see her and to speak with her. It did not fall to his lot to save her, though I know he would freely give his own life to have done it. He admired her; - I would say he loved her deeply, if I thought it possible that you could understand the word. When she was sacrificed, he was thoroughly assured of your guilt. Having lost her, he had but one object left in life, and that was to avenge her and destroy you.'

I saw the villain's nostrils rise and fall convulsively; but I saw no moving at his mouth.

'That man Meltham,' Beckwith steadily pursued, 'was as absolutely certain that you could never elude him in this world, if he devoted himself to your destruction with his utmost fidelity and earnestness, and if he divided the sacred duty with no other duty in life, as he was certain that in achieving it he would be a poor instrument in the hands of Providence, and would do well before Heaven in striking you out from among living men. I am that man, and I thank God that I have done my work!'

If Slinkton had been running for his life from swift-footed savages, a dozen miles, he could not have shown more emphatic signs of being oppressed at heart and labouring for breath, than he showed now, when he looked at the pursuer who had so relentlessly hunted him down.

'You never saw me under my right name before; you see me under my right name now. You shall see me once again in the body, when you are tried for your life. You shall see me once again in the spirit, when the cord is round your neck, and the crowd are crying against you!'

When Meltham had spoken these last words, the miscreant suddenly turned away his face, and seemed to strike his mouth with his open hand. At the same instant, the room was filled with a new and powerful odour, and, almost at the same instant, he broke into a crooked run, leap, start, - I have no name for the spasm, - and fell, with a dull weight that shook the heavy old doors and windows in their frames.

That was the fitting end of him.

When we saw that he was dead, we drew away from the room, and Meltham, giving me his hand, said, with a weary air,

'I have no more work on earth, my friend. But I shall see her again elsewhere.'

It was in vain that I tried to rally him. He might have saved her, he said; he had not saved her, and he reproached himself; he had lost her, and he was broken-hearted.

'The purpose that sustained me is over, Sampson, and there is nothing now to hold me to life. I am not fit for life; I am weak and spiritless; I have no hope and no object; my day is done.'

In truth, I could hardly have believed that the broken man who then spoke to me was the man who had so strongly and so differently impressed me when his purpose was before him. I used such entreaties with him, as I could; but he still said, and always said, in a patient, undemonstrative way, - nothing could avail him, - he was broken-hearted.

He died early in the next spring. He was buried by the side of the poor young lady for whom he had cherished those tender and unhappy regrets; and he left all he had to her sister. She lived to be a happy wife and mother; she married my sister's son, who succeeded poor Meltham; she is living now, and her children ride about the garden on my walking-stick when I go to see her.

Charles Dickens - A Short Biography

Charles Dickens (1812-1870) is regarded by many readers and literary critics to be THE major English novelist of the Victorian Age. He is remembered today as the author of a series of weighty novels which have been translated into many languages and promoted to the rank of World Classics. The latter include, but are not limited to, *The Adventures of Oliver Twist*, *A Tale of Two Cities*, *David Copperfield*, *A Christmas Carol*, *Hard Times*, *Great Expectations* and *The Old Curiosity Shop*.

Birth and Childhood's Hardships

By and large, Charles Dickens's life story is one of somebody who is born and raised in dire straits to become one of the greatest men who have marked human history and thought. It is a perfect example of how the plight of the deprived and the destitute could transform into a precious incentive that pushes them to challenge their circumstances and to unexpectedly excel and shine.

Charles Dickens was born in Portsmouth on February 7th, 1812. His father John Dickens worked as a simple accounting clerk at the Naval Pay Office and the family's pecuniary situation was almost always uneven. When Charles was only two years, the family had to move to London, then later to Chatham. For financial reasons, Charles did not have adequate education. He rather had to leave school at a very young age to work at a polishing and blacking factory. To add insult to injury, Charles's father was imprisoned in 1824 after failing to pay a 40-pound debt.

Charles's experience at the factory played a tremendous role in building the novelist's personality and in deepening his concerns about working children and about the working class in general. Dickens's precocious maturity and the serious responsibilities that he had as a little child left a clear impression on many of his young characters, such as Oliver Twist, David Copperfield and Pip in *Great Expectations*. The hardships that Charles Dickens personally went through made him much interested in defending the poor, in fighting social injustice through exposing its blatant manifestations and in accentuating the importance of having decent work conditions.

Between 1824 and 1827, Dickens's father, who eventually managed to pay his debts, offered Charles the opportunity to attend a private school in North London, the Wellington House Academy. The experience surely enriched the young man's knowledge of the rules of writing and rhetoric and whetted his appetite for 18th-century novels and for the picaresque novels that adorned his father's library. However, during this period, Charles still had to experience another disappointment when his mother refused to spare him the strenuous job at the blacking factory even after the relative improvement of the family's financial situation. The mother's decision had a great psychological impact on young Charles and even influenced his vision of gender roles as he thought that the mother should not be the decision-maker in the family.

Early Publications

Young Charles Dickens occupied numerous jobs and worked hard to learn shorthand. This long and diversified professional experience had a patent impact on his different writings. Indeed, after the blacking factory experience, Dickens first worked as a clerk for attorneys, which allowed him to learn about the legal system and its principles, to become a free-lance reporter for Doctor's Commons Courts in 1829. Later, he even wrote reports for the House of Commons before starting to work for newspapers, magazines and journals.

It was in 1833 that Dickens started writing short stories for a number of literary magazines and journals such as *The Monthly Magazine.* A collection of these texts was later pseudonymously published under the title *Sketches by Boz*. Thanks to Dickens's humor and exceptional writing style, the latter publication was relatively successful, but not as successful as *The Pickwick Papers* whose serial publication sold thousands of copies and raised Dickens to considerable fame. In 1836, he started writing short texts to be published with the humorous illustrations of the famous artist Robert Seymour. These first successes encouraged Dickens to carry on publishing other stories in the form of series. Dickens's next creation was *Oliver Twist* which was published between 1837 and 1839.

It is noteworthy that most of Dickens's novels were published in the form of monthly and weekly chapters which, according to critics and biographers, allowed him to evaluate and adjust his characterizations and plots to meet the expectations of his readership. It was also during this period that Dickens started his long career as a literary magazine editor.

Loves and Marriage

Charles Dickens got married on April 2nd, 1836 to Catherine Thomson Hogarth after one year of engagement. They settled at the famous Furnival's Inn in Holborn, London, before they moved to their home in Bloomsbury. The house was transformed into the Charles Dickens Museum in 1925. Charles and Catherine, who lived there with the first three of their ten children, were joined by Charles's brother Frederick and Catherine's sister Mary. The latter was reported to have had a very special place in Charles's heart. After dying in his own arms in 1837 following a sudden illness, she became a source of inspiration for some of his female characters. After three years of marriage, Dickens's success and rising income made him leave the house for larger and more luxurious estates.

Catherine Hogarth was not Dickens's only love, however. Indeed, biographers report that Dickens's relation with his wife was sandwiched by two other romantic affairs. First, there was Maria Beadnell, a banker's daughter, with whom Dickens fell in love when he was only eighteen years old. The relationship ended three years later when Maria's parents apparently intervened. The other love story that Dickens went through started in 1857 and pushed him to divorce Catherine the following year. It was when Dickens was having a group of young actresses for the staging of his play *The Frozen Deep* that he fell in love with the actress Ellen Ternan who was 27 years younger than him.

Major Achievements

Charles's first success with *The Pickwick Papers* and *Oliver Twist* only pushed him to devote more time and energy to his writing and editorial activities. After publishing *Nicholas Nickleby* between 1838 and 1839, he started a new project in 1840 that he entitled *Master Humphrey's Clock*. The latter is a collection of stories that share the same frame and have recurring characters. It was among this collection that the two major works *The Old Curiosity Shop* and *Barnaby Rudge* were serially published.

After visiting the United States of America in 1842, Dickens developed a rather negative view of the New World which was mainly depicted in his travelogue *American Notes for General Circulation* and also in his picaresque novel *Martin Chuzzlewit*. The latter included very harsh satire of the republic and strongly denounced its institution of slavery. However, the fury that Dickens caused among some American circles was soon quietened with the publication of *A Christmas Carol* in 1843. The book, which is considered by many as the novelist's finest opus, was celebrated both in England and America.

Two other Christmas books followed respectively in 1834 and 1845. They are *The Chimes* and *The Cricket on the Hearth*. During this period,

Dickens also published a new travelogue that he entitled *Pictures from Italy* following his stay in the Mediterranean country. Another Christmas story entitled *The Haunted Man* was published in 1848, which was preceded by *Dombey and Son* (1847) and *The Battle of Life* (1847) and followed by David Copperfield (1849-1850), *Bleak House* (1852-1853) and *Hard Times* (1854).

It was in 1853 that Dickens started organizing public performances in which he presented his literary works. By this time, he also started to collaborate with Wilkie Collins on a number of short stories and plays. *Little Dorrit* started as a monthly serial in 1855 to be finished in 1857. Later, two of Dickens's most valuable works were published: *A Tale of Two Cities* (1859) and *Great Expectations* (1861). They were both published in the weekly periodical, *All the Year Round*, which he founded and edited himself.

Apart from his writings, Dickens's main profitable activity was the public reading of his novels. Along with the money he earned thanks to his successful publications, public readings allowed Dickens to buy his dream house (Gad's Hill Place, Kent), to offer financial help to his parents and brothers and to engage in charitable activities.

Twilight and Death

During the 1860s, Dickens carried on organizing more reading tours. In addition to the many events he had in England, he visited France, the United States, Scotland and Ireland on many an occasion. In 1864, he started his last complete novel, *Our Mutual Friend*. However, by 1865, his health started to waver. This was mainly because of the physical and intellectual exhaustion to which he subjected himself. Furthermore, Dickens was psychologically traumatized in 1865 following a train crash. He was with his beloved Ellen Ternan on their way back from Paris when their train derailed to cause a big number of casualties. Although Dickens was able to collect his courage and managed to help the wounded and comfort them, the picture of the disaster affected him greatly and could never be erased from his mind.

For health reasons, Dickens cancelled many of his programmed readings between 1868 and 1870. On April 22nd, 1869, he had a stroke. The latter was followed by a second stroke on June 8th, 1870, while he was working on his novel *The Mystery of Edwin Drood* which would remain unfinished. The next day, he passed away. Charles Dickens today rests in The Poets' Corner of Westminster Abbey.